Praise for We Are Li

"An ingenious and highly original composition. What emerges is a beautiful, soulful, rich, and relevant portrait of what people are looking for when they reject science, of what people can do to themselves, just to stay together, to be part of a herd, a group, a 'we.'"
Jury, Libris Literature Prize

"This novel has a good chance of becoming the most remarkable and formally innovative debut novel of the spring. It's a remarkable novel, and, despite its oppressive subject, a true pleasure to read."
Der Standard

"Convincingly, Gerda Blees finds her meticulously narrated way through the minefield of fashionable trends."
Frankfurter Allgemeine Zeitung

"A penetrating psychological text that plumbs the depths of human deception of ourselves and others."
Die Presse

"An excellent novel. The stunning final chapter will leave readers gasping for air."
VPRO Gids

"The changing perspective allows Blees to zoom in, zoom out, conceal, and reveal. It's a game loaded with unexpected tension. You're taken by surprise time and again."
NRC Handelsblad

"It's nice when a writer has the guts to do something different, but it's priceless when this unconventionality has added value and leads to a unique novel."
De Volkskrant

"It's brilliant how Blees manages to turn the 'we are …' every chapter starts with into the book's main theme. You feel that you're holding something remarkable in your hands."
Trouw

"She sets the tone with ever-changing perspectives, sometimes drily comical, often also touching and very human; she colors the story of the people who want to live on light and air in an entirely novel way."
Het Parool

"Blees masters the art of taking the reader by the hand and leading them past successive stages of concern, outrage, and resignation. She subtly calls into question the judgments we pass on idealistic people such as the novel's protagonists, and she allows us to empathize with people we initially thought we'd never be able to relate to."
Tzum

"The stream of consciousness that runs through Elisabeth's demented mother's head is brilliant."
Knack

"It sounds crazy but the talented Blees pulls it off: her story alternates between the perspectives of, for instance, a slow juicer, a cello, a demented mother,

and the crime scene. An unconventional reading experience."
De Morgen

"A dramatic but humorous story about how people can lose themselves in an ideal."
HP/De Tijd

"A pageturner that isn't just suspenseful, but also very relevant and exquisitely narrated."
FM4 (Austria)

"Original and astonishing!"
MDR Kultur

We Are Light

Gerda Blees

We Are Light

Translated from the Dutch
by Michele Hutchison

WORLD EDITIONS
New York, London, Amsterdam

Published in the USA in 2023 by World Editions LLC, New York
Published in the UK in 2023 by World Editions Ltd., London

World Editions
New York/London/Amsterdam

Wij zijn licht © Gerda Blees, 2020
English translation copyright © Michele Hutchison, 2023
Author portrait © Bartjan de Bruijn

World Editions is committed to a sustainable future. Papers
used by World Editions meet the FSC standards of certification.

This book is a work of fiction. Any resemblance to actual
persons, living or dead, or actual events is purely coincidental.

Library of Congress Cataloging in Publication Data is available

ISBN 978-1-64286-127-3

First published as *Wij zijn licht* in the Netherlands in 2020 by
Uitgeverij Podium, Amsterdam

This publication has been made possible with financial
support from the Dutch Foundation for Literature

N ederlands
letterenfonds
dutch foundation
for literature

All rights reserved. No part of this publication may be reproduced,
stored in or introduced into a retrieval system, or transmitted, in
any form, or by any means (electronic, mechanical, photocopying,
recording or otherwise) without the prior written permission of
the publisher.

Company: worldeditions.org
Facebook: @WorldEditionsInternationalPublishing
Instagram: @WorldEdBooks
TikTok: @worldeditions_tok
Twitter: @WorldEdBooks
YouTube: World Editions

1

We are night. We bring darkness, drunkenness, fighting cats, sleep, sleeplessness, sex, and death. People wanting to die in peace, without fuss or ado, often choose to do so in our—the night's—company, while the about-to-be-bereaved slumber on. Here we see many cancer patients, people with heart and lung disease, and the exhausted elderly, breathe their last breath, almost unnoticed, at night. But we are no strangers to less peaceful ways of dying: fights, traffic accidents, murder, and manslaughter. You wouldn't want to hear about the awful things we've witnessed, not even if you like horror films and have a strong stomach, and nor do we want to talk about it. There are more interesting ways for people to die, such as the case of the woman who has our attention at the present moment. Here, the familiar elements of a peaceful death coincide with disturbingly abnormal circumstances.

Normal: a sitting room with 1990s furniture, tasteless ornaments on the walls—large colourful metal butterflies, old musical instruments of varying sizes—and, in this room, a sleeping woman with wispy grey hair, so thin and weak that her heart could give out at any moment. Next to her a relative, her sister judging from the shape of her face, clasping both hands in her own as though she's trying to keep this near-dead human alive.

Abnormal: everything else, but particularly the fact that the sisters are lying on inflatable beds in the middle of the room, and the presence of the other people: a middle-aged man and a somewhat younger woman, watching from a red sofa. They have almost as little flesh on their bones as the dying woman; their cheeks have caved in, their eyes are sunk deep in their sockets. Although they don't appear to be on the brink of death, we can see their skeletons jutting through their skin. And the way they are breathing, as though they are afraid of taking in too much air at once, tells us that they may not be dead, but they are not entirely alive either. Maybe that's why they are sitting there with the windows closed, in the stuffy leftover heat of a summer's day, and they haven't switched on the lights, so that only a thin orange beam from a streetlight outside the house falls through a chink in the curtains into the room, cutting diagonally across the beds of the two recumbent women.

We've seen these airbeds here before. Usually there are four of them. The dying woman, her sister, and the two other people all sleep on them next to each other on the floor. Not much else happens. They're no night owls, aside from the woman on the sofa, who often lies staring up at the ceiling, eyes wide-open, her stomach making rumbling and churning noises beneath her fleece blanket. From time to time, a grimace appears on her face. She balls her fists. She bites on her knuckles. She sucks her bottom lip. Sometimes she falls asleep after a couple of hours anyway, but often she crawls out quietly from under her blanket and creeps to the toilet to drink some water from the tap, repeating this every hour or so.

We get the impression that she's hungry, though we've never been able to catch her taking a nocturnal trip to the fridge, unlike a lot of people who can't sleep due to the gurgling emptiness in their bellies. In the three years we've seen her like this, we've only seen her in the kitchen once. She stood in front of the slow juicer for a long time, stroking its side as though it were a gentle, sweet pet, and then kneeled at the fridge, pressing her forehead to its door. She sat there for more than an hour without moving. Then she rested her fingers on the handle. We saw the muscles and tendons of her hand tense as she squeezed with all her might. Her elbow lifted slightly, and she let go. She stood up. Faltered. Grabbed the worktop. Leaned forward, head between her knees. Straightened up again, slower now. She took a step. Her eyes roved around the monochrome darkness and paused at an apple in the fruit bowl on the counter. She went over to it but didn't pick it up. She leaned forward, brought her nose right up to it, and stared at the apple.

If we'd have been able to speak we would have shouted at her, "Eat then, woman, eat! Nobody's stopping you." But she didn't eat. When she managed to pry herself away from the apple and tiptoe back to the sitting room, she came upon the oldest of the four— the one now dying—awake, eyes open. She stood there, startled, caught in her housemate's gaze. Her eyes were expressionless, showing neither recognition, nor disapproval, nor reassurance. Nothing. And in that same expressionless manner, the staring eyes closed again. Our hungry friend let her shoulders sink, slowly continued on her way, and lay back down on her airbed, waiting for day to break.

As the earth's night, we are not easily unsettled, but this we do find remarkable—that people in a country such as this would voluntarily suffer from hunger, with food literally within hand's reach. As though wanting to protest against the abundance granted them.

And now death has arrived in hunger's wake, not for our chronic insomniac, but for her housemate.

"She's gone," says the sister, sitting upright on her airbed now, still clutching the dead woman's hands. "I felt her pass … It was so smooth, so beautiful. Really special, don't you think?"

She looks at the other two, her eyes enquiring. They are breathing even more cautiously than earlier. "Did you see that? Did you see how calm she became when I took her hands? She could finally let go … let herself go. Beautiful that it happened like that, right? That we didn't try to hold her back. Right? Petrus? Muriel?"

Petrus and Muriel don't move a muscle. Their faces remain expressionless as their eyes dart around, searching for something they can't find in the shadowy darkness. Finally Muriel says, "Beautiful, yes."

"What about you, Petrus? What are you feeling now? Anything to share?"

Petrus closes his eyes and shakes his head as though plagued by an insect he daren't slap away. His forehead is shiny with sweat.

"Never mind," the sister says. "It's difficult to truly open up to everything you're feeling at such an intense moment. It's difficult. I understand that, really I do."

Without saying anything, Petrus gets up from the sofa, opens the back door, and goes into the garden.

"Alright, Petrus," the sister says. And to Muriel: "It's okay. Just a bit of psychological resistance. Doesn't matter. It'll come later. Elisabeth is the most important person now. Can you pass me the phone? And the GP's number? I think it's better if I stay with her awhile. I think she'd appreciate that."

Muriel gets up, goes to a rucksack in the corner of the room, takes out a mobile phone, and gives it to the sister. "Just have to look up the number." She sits down at the table and opens a laptop.

"That's kind of you, Muriel," the sister says. "Very kind. It's lovely that we're together, that we were all together with Elisabeth. She must have felt it. She *is* feeling it. Because I can sense she's still in the room. Can't you?"

"Huh," Muriel says in a flat tone.

"That she's still with us: Elisabeth. Actually I can feel her presence quite strongly. But of course I am her sister."

Muriel squeezes her eyes shut and frowns. Then she opens her eyes. The blue-white light of the laptop makes her face appear even more ghostly. "Yes," she says, "yes, I can feel her too, yes." She nods at Elisabeth's body and looks at the screen again. "It says here to call the out-of-hours service at night." She begins to read out numbers and the sister types them into the mobile phone.

"Yes, hello. Melodie van Hellingen speaking. I'm calling about my sister."

From here we fast-forward a bit, analogous to the experience of anyone who has stayed awake all night—at first the time goes slowly but then suddenly it is morning.

A discussion unfolds with the out-of-hours receptionist. The receptionist says she'll send the duty doctor, but Melodie thinks it would be better if her own GP came to certify the death because this was an unusual case, her sister, in terms of her medical file, but also because of the emotional bond, and if their own GP really can't come, it's important that the duty doctor reads the whole case file, and on the other end of the line, we see the receptionist roll her eyes and ask Melodie in an extremely friendly tone whether she can briefly tell her how exactly her sister died, and Melodie says it was all very beautiful because Elisabeth was able to let go at last, because life had been a battle for her, and as the receptionist says "hm, hm" and "yes" she glances at the patient's date of birth and types up something about a muddled story and "possible suicide" then she says to Melodie that unfortunately the duty doctor will have to come and he won't have access to the medical file, but that she can count on his professionalism, and all in all Melodie finds this a cold way of going about things, an impersonal system in which rules matter more than people, but the receptionist doesn't have time to hear Melodie out, the lights are flashing for other incoming calls, so she says goodbye in a firm but friendly voice, hangs up, and completes her notes for the doctor who will come to examine Elisabeth van Hellingen's body.

Melodie has a bad feeling about the phone call, she says to Muriel, and to Petrus, who has come back into the room; she doesn't like being treated in such a businesslike manner, certainly not after something so special, so intimate, but also so sad has taken place, and she's saying this without knowing how unpleasantly she's going to be treated later, because the system involves rules and procedures that your regular man or woman on the street has no idea of, and the duty doctor, who has rung on the doorbell by now and has come inside to examine the dead woman, carefully follows the procedure prescribed by law, and with little empathy, Melodie thinks, because he insists she turns on the light and that all three housemates leave the sitting room so he can look at the body without being disturbed, despite Melodie telling him that bright light and the absence of her housemates is unpleasant for Elisabeth, and on top of this he cuts her off when she tries to answer his questions; he doesn't want to know anything about their childhood and the weak constitution Elisabeth was born with, or their sick mother with whom she had a good moment of connection recently, he is only interested in their diet, and when Elisabeth last ate or drank anything and whether she might have taken mind-altering substances at all, and finally he says that unfortunately he has too many doubts about whether she died of natural causes, and it doesn't matter how often Melodie says that it all happened very naturally—backed up by the nods of the two other housemates who have taken up position on the red sofa again—he can only go by his own observations, and what he observes is an unpleasant, suffocating atmosphere and seriously low bodyweight, both in terms of the deceased but also her housemates, and he has too many questions about the circumstances of Ms Van Hellingen's death, her no longer being in the full bloom of youth but also not nearly old enough to just suddenly die, and they can shout as loudly as they like, they can jump up and down, but if there is any cause for doubt it is his legal duty to inform the local coroner, who must then alert the police, and without listening to any of their further objections, he goes into the garden to phone the coroner, bringing upon himself, like the receptionist earlier, accusations of coldness when he returns to the sitting room.

Wrongly, we think; the locum may have a deep furrow in the middle of his forehead, not because he is cold or hard but because he takes things seriously, and that's why we'd rather use the word "unflappable" to describe the way he allows Melodie's protests to slide off his back and sits down on the sofa with the three bereaved, two of them paralysed and one unutterably outraged, to wait for the police to arrive and take over the case, and as he goes on his way to the next house call and the incident begins to take shape in his mind as an interesting case study for the locum's lunch next week, the detective who has been sent along with two uniformed colleagues stays behind to keep an eye on everything until the coroner arrives, which unfortunately is a long wait—it seems that several suspicious deaths have occurred in the last few hours—and not until the coroner has arrived for a second examination of the body, and, despite another round of protests from Melodie, the group has left the room, can the detective, after consulting the specialist medical examiner and the assistant prosecutor, figure out whether a criminal investigation needs to be launched, while her two colleagues remain upstairs to listen to Melodie and give her the opportunity—quickly then, very quickly—to call her father and bring him up to date on the situation, while the duty detective, after interviewing the three survivors, goes downstairs to make the necessary phone calls to the assistant prosecutor to ask whether the housemates should be detained, and if so, based on which article of law, and as soon as they are in agreement, she goes back upstairs with a cool, if not to say frosty, expression on her face, to apprehend the housemates on suspicion of culpable homicide and to read them their rights, and after that there is a phase of upheaval as they wait for a third police officer, and after he has arrived to take away the third suspect, Muriel, Petrus, and Melodie are driven to the police station, each in a separate car, as the detective and the coroner remain behind at the crime scene, and we would have liked to have stayed a little longer with the three detainees, and with Muriel in particular, who, all other emotions aside, is still suffering from gnawing hunger, but before everything continues, forced on by the unrelenting revolutions of the earth, we begin to withdraw behind the western horizon, where other interesting deaths and sleepless humans await us.

2

We are the crime scene. Not so long ago we were just a house, hardly different from all the other houses in the neighbourhood, even with our unusual inhabitants and our appearance, which differed only slightly from the norm. But ever since somebody died inside us and the police came, we've been called the crime scene.

"Can you send someone along to keep an eye on the crime scene?" the police woman asked on the telephone, after our inhabitants, three living and one dead, had been taken away. A quarter of an hour later, another police car pulled up in front of our door, and since this morning all kinds of people have been walking around who just can't stop talking about us: crime scene this and crime scene that, and will you come to the crime scene, and I'm at the crime scene.

It's a dubious honour, this new name. The people who come here are not exactly polite. Without asking the inhabitants' permission they touch our surfaces with their plastic-gloved hands and their swabs, they rummage around our cupboards and place objects belonging to us in transparent plastic bags. On the one hand all this attention is flattering, but on the other, it feels a bit invasive. And the way they just left our front door open; they did put red-and-white tape across it, but still. All that air just freely coming in and flowing out again. Admittedly, it's often rather stuffy and oppressive inside, but we're used to that.

Nobody knows what a house without people looks like from the inside, but these people come close. They are in us, but they are also outside of us. They walk around in the coagulated version of us that came into existence when one of our inhabitants stopped living and the other three were taken away.

They're out of place here, these people. They're too big, too broad, too noisy. Our stairs can barely cope with such stamping, heavy bodies, not the weight and not the sound either. They could be a bit more careful with us, if you think that we're the place where the answer can be found. At least that's what he says, the man with the moustache and the belly —a belly like we haven't seen in years—who is standing in front of our open door wearing civvies, next to a grumpy-looking woman, while inside the people in uniform are going about their business with rubber gloves and plastic bags. "The answer can be found at the crime scene, that's what I always say. But if you don't mind me sharing my gut feeling, I don't think there's much of a case here, just going on the feel of the place."

He sniffs at the air, while his eyes run up our frontage, inducing a spontaneous bout of embarrassment regarding the colours of our door and our window frames: orange, yellow, purple, and green. Not colours we would have chosen ourselves, but no one ever asked our opinion on matters concerning our appearance or decoration. He and the woman stare at the five red plates next to the door. The top one has SOUND & LOVE COMMUNE written on it in orange letters, and underneath there's a stave with a couple of music notes. Under this, four different nameplates with the names of our inhabitants, also in orange. MELODIE VAN HELLINGEN. ELISABETH VAN HELLINGEN. PETRUS ZWARTS. MURIEL DE VREE. The names are listed in descending order of age, except for Melodie's, which is at the top, even though she's younger than Elisabeth.

The woman writes something in her notepad. "Sound and Love," she says. "Fine kind of love, letting your own sister starve to death."

"Hmm," the man replies. "That's not like you, Liz. We don't judge, we investigate."

He holds up the red-and-white tape for her so she can pass under it, then follows her into the hall. A man coming down the stairs with plastic bags nods in greeting and continues into the sitting room.

"Let's start by taking a look around," Liz says.

She begins at the front door. The little curtains, the tear-shaped glass object dangling on a fishing line in front of the pane of glass, the wind chimes hung with sellotape from the side of the ceiling lamp so that the bars jingle whenever anyone opens or closes the front door. The yellow hall walls. We remember Melodie painting our walls that colour with Petrus.

"The colour of the sun," she'd said. "It gives energy."

Each wall of the toilet is a different colour, and the ceiling yet another—everyone could pick one. A birthday calendar with crayon drawings of angels hangs on the inside of the door. No birthdays this month. There are hardly any names in the rest of the calendar, maybe ten in all, all of them in Melodie's handwriting. She'd said, "I'd appreciate it if we could decide together who we put on the calendar. If you read the name while on the toilet, you absorb some of that person's energy."

Liz and the man move on deeper into us. They read us, they listen to us. If we had arms we'd cross them protectively in front of our rooms to hide our most intimate parts from their alien hands and eyes. They inspect the butterflies on the sitting room wall. With fat fingers he strums the strings of the instruments hanging in two rows of four. Four viola da gambas, four lutes. Two airbeds are still on the floor in the centre of the room, two others stand upright against two tall shelving units.

"So this is how they sleep," the fat man says. He squats next to one of the airbeds and presses on it; it bounces a little. "Spartan. I wonder whether they get up at four thirty every day too."

But they don't; we can testify to that. Daylight rules in this house. When it enters the room in the morning through the curtains, the inhabitants gradually open their eyes and begin to move around in silence. They fold up their sheets and their blue fleece blankets and prop up their airbeds between the shelving units.

"Anyone want juice?" Muriel usually asks, but Melodie prefers to wait a while, tune in first. They fetch their meditation cushions from the pile next to the sofa, place them in a ring on the floor, sit down cross-legged, and close their eyes. Melodie says they should all turn their attention to their breathing, relaxing deeper with each exhalation, then anyone who feels the urge can start by humming a note. Melodie is always the one who feels the urge first. After she's begun, the others join in, each a different note so it seems as though they are trying to reach some kind of harmony. Sometimes Melodie says "stop." Then they have to listen harder, tune in better. When Melodie is satisfied she takes one of the other's hands and that person does the same until they are all holding hands, and then we see them shift about awkwardly and frown, and the sound continues to swell and sometimes they secretly peek at each other through squinted eyes and after a few minutes the humming gradually dies out. It doesn't sound awful but it's not pleasant either. You can't call it music. Sound is a better word, which probably explains that sign saying *SOUND & LOVE COMMUNE*.

Melodie has the patience of an angel, at least she thinks so. "It's very difficult, dealing with all your emotions," she says to the others when they cry or get angry or don't feel like talking. "Sometimes I get the feeling I know more about what's going on inside you than you do yourselves. It feels like quite a responsibility, you know." And then her eyes begin to tear up but they don't usually really cry.

"Would you check these first? Then we can get going with the contents," Liz, gesturing at the two laptops, says to the man dealing with the belongings in the living room. We gulp. Two of our most intimate data carriers just grabbed from the table and bagged up. They've spent a lot of time on these two computers. You can still see their sweat on the keys. At first, when the other three had only just moved in with Melodie, there was just one, used exclusively by Melodie, but after a while Petrus started asking for some time on it, and then Muriel suddenly wanted the same. A second laptop arrived and a pink sheet of paper on the noticeboard above the dining table, which is still there. Liz takes a picture of it.

Who can use the laptops:

	Big laptop	Little laptop
10am–noon	Melodie	Petrus
2pm–4pm	Muriel	Melodie
4pm–6pm	Melodie	Petrus
8pm–9pm	Petrus	Muriel

Melodie needed the most time because she writes the text for the website and the newsletter and she has a blog where she writes about personal stuff.

"'Melodie shares'—do you think that's a good title for a blog?" she'd asked the others and the others thought it was.

"The victim's not here," says Liz, "on the laptop roster."

"Maybe she was computer illiterate? Or mentally impaired?"

"No, there's nothing like that in the report."

But if you heard the way Melodie spoke to Elisabeth you might think she was. There are barely any traces of her left in us, besides her crayon drawings.

"Look here, Elisabeth," Melodie had said, sliding two sheets of music staves across the table to her, one of them filled in with notes and the other blank. "Maybe you'd like to go over these notes in crayon?"

And when Elisabeth didn't reply. "Go on. It'll do you good." At which point Elisabeth took the crayons and the music sheets and began colouring, her head bent over the paper, the tip of her tongue sticking out of her mouth.

If anyone were to ask us what her voice actually sounded like, Elisabeth's voice, we'd have to admit to having forgotten. She spoke so little that it drove the others crazy at times. But when she did try to say something, she was interrupted before she could finish.

"*I thank the sun for her infinite energy,*" Liz reads from a crayoned note on the noticeboard. "*The world is a place of abundance. Love is my birthright. There is always enough.*" She sniffs. "Except for food. Have you already looked in the fridge, Ton?"

The man with the belly, Ton's his name then, gets up at once and goes to the kitchen. "Not much to see here," he calls out, as Liz goes through the pile of newspapers and magazines on the dining table. *Green Living, The Institute for Alternative Medicine, Happinez, Fighting Consumerism.* She straightens the pile and goes after Ton.

"There is a slow juicer. And enough celery to make some delicious and nutritious celery juice," she comments, inspecting the contents of the fridge over his shoulder. "Unbelievable. It makes me so angry."

"Yes, you can't survive on that, can you?" says Ton.

"You can survive for quite a while on a couple of celery sticks a day," Liz replies. "Believe me."

"Strange folk. Really strange," says Ton. "Although I do wonder whether we can make a case here. Going on that briefing, it's all rather *lean*."

"Jesus, Ton. That woman is dead, you know. The fact there's no gun lying around doesn't mean nothing happened. You should know that. You with your *we don't judge*. Just because the public prosecutor is a woman and didn't agree with you on that last case. You're just a cranky ass."

Ton holds up his hands as though he's under fire. "Whoa, whoa, whoa, Liesbeth. No need for that. I'm just wondering whether any criminal offenses have been committed here. It all looks very sad but it seems to me more something for social services." He turns and looks at her. "Quick look upstairs? Or do you want a cigarette first to calm down?"

"No, thank you," says Liz. She turns and goes ahead of him into the hall. The stairs sigh and creak beneath their feet.

"Oh. Nice and hot up here," Ton says. "They could have opened a window."

Our top floor has enough space for a family with 2.4 children but there's just one single bed which is covered in piles of sheet music. Apart from that, lots of bookcases, a clothes horse draped with dry laundry, a cupboard containing photo albums. Melodie's cello is in one of the rooms. We miss that sometimes. That was real music, what she produced with the cello in the olden days. She could play beautifully, particularly when she was sad. But Ton and Liz are more interested in our recent past. They check the bathroom, look inside the pedal bin. We can already tell you they won't find any signs of sexual activity or drugs use inside. No condoms, no regular medicines, not even paracetamol. There is a cupboard filled with homeopathic medicine, environmentally friendly cosmetics, and Bach's rescue remedy.

Liz pauses in front of a yellow note stuck into one corner of the mirror.

We are light
We are love
We are sound everywhere
We are cells filled with life
We are nothing
We are the universe

Underneath this, another note: *Together = not alone!*

Melodie always says this in front of the mirror. She looks at herself and forms the words with her mouth, without making a sound.

We often think about the word *alone*. As a terraced house we've only ever experienced sharing a wall with another house on each side. There are always the three of us, even though we can never experience what goes on inside the other two houses. And we don't feel the need to either. Sharing walls with the other two, knowing that we don't have to be completely alone in the world, like a detached house or a farm, that's enough, to be honest.

But it seems more complicated with people when it comes to loneliness. It's not just the quantity of the company or the physical distance from one person to the next that determines the degree of loneliness. I guess there are care homes that could tell you all kinds of stuff, if we're to believe Melodie's stories about her mother. Where our inhabitants are concerned, once the other three moved in with Melodie, once they lived together, the four of them, the loneliness contained between our walls seemed to quadruple. Melodie used to hum her monotonous tune on her own, later there were four voices. While she used to complain either internally or on the phone about the disconnected state society was in, now they talked about that together. While she used to look in the mirror and smile in an attempt to like herself, now they smiled at each other and into their phone cameras together. And though they often said out loud how much they liked each other, though they'd planned weekly slots to tell each other why they were so happy together, even we, just a simple 1980s house, could tell from their faces that half of what they were saying wasn't true. And every day someone lay down on the sofa and cried, or kicked their feet black and blue against the outside wall.

We are the crime scene, but which crime? you may ask yourself. The police are looking for signs of negligence, of pressure to follow a starvation diet, of neglect. We have a different crime in mind. We suspect the inhabitants of the Sound & Love Commune of having trapped each other in a cage of loneliness. And Elisabeth freed herself.

3

We are your daily bread. The most normal bread there is, regular wholemeal, baked on an industrial scale, machine cut, each slice wrapped in plastic to be doled out in those institutions that keep the world free of infirmity, illness, and aggression: nursing homes, hospitals, prisons. And that's how we found ourselves on the custody officer's breakfast trolley in a police station's cell complex, and after that, on a small table in Muriel's cell. She's the last person we'd have expected to see here. She was always such a sweet, obedient child. She gave us up years ago but when the custody officer came in just now and asked whether she wanted brown or white, she'd said "brown" before she had time to think, after which he'd placed a nice brown slice on her table, and now she's sitting on her bed giving us a despairing look, while the officer waits for her to answer his question about whether she'd prefer milk- or dark-chocolate sprinkles on it.

"I'll give you some extra water anyway. We usually manage to keep it cool in here but with this weather it's hard to get rid of the heat."

Individually packed slices. Frowned upon by many, not just Muriel. Bread has been sent to the doghouse. We, the bread that centuries of God-fearing

Christians have prayed for, are losing ground every-where. We made man mighty, literally, and now we're being cast aside like old news. They say we contain too much gluten, and the wrong carbohy-drates, whatever those might be. They say we dam-age intestinal walls and cause fluctuations in energy levels. Human memory is short, as we keep seeing. Not so long ago we still made a difference. People died of hunger if there was a shortage of us, and they revolted on our behalf. Social activists built bread factories to make us affordable and available to the poor.

All of it, forgotten. And the respect we'd been af-forded: melted away, like snow in the sun. Un-healthy is what we're called now, and unnatural. Loveless, just because we were made in a factory. As if people in white hairnets working on a conveyor belt couldn't put any love into their work. As if our ingredients don't come from the same plants that grow in the earth. As if the parameters of our pro-duction process aren't calculated with infinite pa-tience and care and refined to create the best taste and structure and the longest shelf life. As if dozens of people on tasting panels haven't tasted us before-hand and then tasted us again until they came to the unanimous conclusion that we taste best this way. And as if the machines that make us don't do so with a precision that far exceeds human powers of perception. In short, as if we couldn't be the re-sult of the genuine love and passion of the people and machines who produced us.

And we don't know if you've noticed but coinci-dentally it seems to be precisely those people who pay lip service to the universal power of love who then come up with an endless list of things that are lacking in that love, that are flawed and wrong, like us, guileless bread from a guileless factory. A society that no longer reveres its daily bread begins to lose its grip on reality, if you ask us.

Thank God this troubling development hasn't yet reached the institutions that bring order to society, and it is due to this that we have been reunited with Muriel today.

Our reunion is awkward. The custody officer, who looks like a healthy consumer of cereals and wheat, is waiting for the answer to his question of what kind of chocolate sprinkles she'd like, but Muriel is still doing sums. We see her eyes move around all over the place as she adds up, takes away, and multiplies. She already had that as a kid, the compulsion to count and calculate. After she'd learned the numbers up to twenty, she'd often count all the sunflower seeds on her crust out loud, or all the chocolate sprinkles that had fallen next to it on her plate. The chocolate sprinkles must have been at her grandmother's house because her parents never gave her sugary things to put on her bread, they were quite strict about that. And this proved fatal for us, because it's often the ones with the strict upbringing who decide to give us up later on.

But today Muriel's internal calculation settles in favour of the chocolate sprinkles.

"Dark chocolate please," she says.

"And tea or coffee?"

"Tea."

"With sugar?"

"Yes please," says Muriel. "Wait … no, yes please."

The custody officer places the objects of her desire next to us on the little table and she sits down on the ground to arrange everything as she wants it. We're directly to the left, to our right the packet of sprinkles, parallel to this the sachet of sugar, and all the way to the right, the cup of tea, with two cups of water lined up behind it.

She doesn't hear the rest of what the officer says— that she'll be able to speak to her lawyer soon but unfortunately not to her housemates, and that she can use the shower if she wants. All her attention is taken up by the display before her, and in particular by us.

What is she thinking of doing? Does she really think she can resist us now we're so close by? Our little cement mixer, as her mother used to say, half lovingly, half condemningly, because Muriel liked to take a sip of milk with every well-chewed mouthful so that we passed into her gullet soaked in milk. She was a real bread-eater. How she enjoyed us, and in such quantities. Three slices at breakfast, four at school, and another two in the evening, toasted with cheese, before swimming practice. The way she churned us around in her mouth with her tongue! What a joy!

And later, when she'd learned that you should chew each bite thirty-six times before swallowing it, we were turned to pulp. She kept this up for eighteen months until she got a boyfriend who laughed in her face when she told him. After that she ate us like she used to, and her love for us was just as strong. No one chewed us with so much care, no one produced as much saliva as she did, particularly not after she'd moved into halls in her second year of Business Studies and replaced peanut butter at breakfast with butter and dark chocolate sprinkles.

"Butter goes to your butt," her mother said, because that's what her parents were like. On the scales each day, no sugar, no butter, only ever wholemeal bread. Nothing wrong with that, of course, although it was quite Calvinist. It's alright to pile fat and sugar on us sometimes, it makes life more pleasant. But Muriel wasn't at all the type to have to worry about her butt. She had a fast metabolism, she was the kind of girl who got anaemic when she didn't eat enough.

She must be anaemic now, she's so skinny. She hasn't touched us yet, and we're starting to get impatient. We were made to connect with a person's body, not to slowly mould away in plastic. We contain enough preservatives to stay fresh for a while, but in this heat, not that long.

"So, you don't want to shower?" the officer asks, still in the door opening.

Muriel looks up. "Um. Yes please," she says and we catch a glimpse of the inside of her mouth, where we'll hopefully find ourselves soon.

"Alright, I'll come and get you in a bit."

And with those words the officer disappears. Finally, we're alone with her. She'll give us all her attention, at least. We feel her longing but also her mistrust. And then we remember the voice of that woman, Melodie, the woman she was living with when she gave us up.

"We're all free to eat what we want but bread does

drain a lot of energy from your body. And I don't think it will help the clarity of your voice, Muriel. Perhaps that's one of the reasons things aren't working out. You could see what effect it has by doing without for a while."

The clarity of her voice. What nonsense. Everyone knows that Muriel can't sing. She was born with many talents but singing was not one of them, as her mother always said. Unbelievable that Melodie is blaming us for that. But she wasn't a bread-eater, never had been. She'd always only picked at us and we weren't that upset when she cut us out.

We have missed Muriel, though, and she us. She looks like she needs us more than ever at the moment. So skinny, so tired, so frightened. Lining her stomach would help so much. But doubt has a stranglehold on her. The paralysing thought that everything depends on whether she eats us or not. That everything will be lost if she eats us. Oh sweetheart. We're only bread. No one ever died from eating bread. Honestly, they didn't.

Muriel rests her hand on our wrapper, and presses. We feel the warmth of her fingers through the plastic. She brings us to her nose and sniffs. Then she puts us down, picks up the little packet of sprinkles and rubs the grains between her fingers. Now she'll eat us. Any moment now.

But she doesn't. Something else wins out, probably Melodie's voice, saying all the things that are wrong with us. Instead of eating us, Muriel takes a sip of tea and begins to sing softly in her quavering, unsteady voice.

We are light
We are love
We are sound everywhere
We are cells filled with life
We are nothing
We are the universe

It must be because of Melodie that she's singing instead of eating. She caused Muriel to give us up, after all. Everyone was free to eat what they wanted as long as it was what Melodie thought best. Just after Muriel moved in with her, she stopped washing down her food because drinking milk was suddenly unhealthy. Next we were kicked off the breakfast table, replaced with oats, and "nice fresh fruit" as Melodie called it—there were enough nutrients in that.

Finally she began to criticise our flavour.

"You can taste all the stuff that's been added," Melodie said. "Bread's generally not that healthy, but if you're going to eat it, sourdough's best. And organic. At the end of the day it's all energy you're absorbing. I was wondering whether we shouldn't switch to a raw food diet. Not sure how you all feel about it."

We could feel that the saliva in Muriel's mouth didn't agree at all. But she did eventually give us up. About a year after Muriel moved in with Melodie she ate her last sandwich, and we haven't seen her since. That's to say, we did see her from the supermarket shelves—she stopped going to the supermarket too in fact—we saw her looking at us longingly when she was shopping with her housemates, and sometimes she'd press her fingers into our wrappers as she passed. But we were never allowed to touch the inside of her mouth again.

Muriel has stopped singing, her focus is on us again. Our appearance isn't the issue, we're sure of that. Our colour, shape, taste: within the range of perfect to extremely perfect. Muriel has been lucky enough to have been given one of our more perfect examples. A smooth, light, elastic texture, a nice crust, not too brown, not too pale, not too limp, and not too crusty. A really nice healthy slice of bread.

But Muriel still doesn't touch us. Instead she takes another sip of tea and begins to count silently. We see her mouth moving: one hundred, ninety-nine, ninety-eight. Her hands rest on her belly.

Time passes and Muriel leaves us untouched. She counts, sings, rocks, takes alternate tiny sips of her cooling tea and the extra water she was given. She lies down on her bed with her back to us. She wants us but she doesn't, and after just over an hour, the healthy consumer of cereal foods returns to say that she can shower in five minutes, and that in an hour she can talk to someone from mental health services, and after that her lawyer.

"Okay," says Muriel, nodding.

The man looks at us. "You don't want your bread?"

She squeezes her eyes shut and it takes her an immense effort to shake her head. One single, quick shake.

"I'll take it away then."

Muriel watches us go with regret, and we're sorry to leave her behind. We imagine her crying out "No, wait," right after the door shuts behind us, biting her lip and adding, "Maybe later."

Maybe later. That's what she'll say to the closed door, because she knows she needs us, however fervently she counts down from a hundred to zero.

As we are carried through the corridor, away from Muriel, we daydream. We think of the soft warmth that can suddenly break out in her mouth. The way we would be chewed, mixed with melted sprinkles, moved around by her tongue, and swallowed, through the pinkish-red throat and into her small, narrow body. We'll fill the emptiness of her stomach with our sticky gluten, our fortifying fibre, our mind-strengthening carbohydrates. It's going to happen, very soon. It must. Today she has resisted us, but we'll be back.

4

We are the neighbours. To say that the entire street is in uproar would be an exaggeration, but a sense of disquiet lingers around the houses. It's not often that a criminal investigation takes place in our neighbourhood, with police tape and agents in uniforms with holstered guns who come and ask us questions. In principle we're a respectable neighbourhood. Lively but respectable. Absolutely not criminal, in general. So, yeah, it has created a stir, what happened. It makes you think.

Number 42 found out about it first because he always gets up at five in the morning to get to Groningen ahead of the traffic jams, amazing that he manages to keep it up, crazy, but whatever, about quarter past five he saw three police cars drive away, and after that they came and put the tape around the house. After that, other police cars drove past and the police began to walk in and out of the house and it was clear that something terrible had happened. We thought maybe a family tragedy, or rather a commune tragedy, because with so many police officers the first thing you think of is a serious crime. Maybe that man with the red hair had finally totally lost it and done in one of the three women, or himself, or everyone, but then it got out somehow that one of the two older women had kicked the bucket, and it seems that there were people who said they hoped it was Melodie, the one who talks all the time and never lets other people finish, which some of us find quite annoying, but such comments were immediately cut short because of course it's not alright to wish death on anybody, and certainly not because of them being annoying. Everyone has their likes and dislikes, but you wouldn't wish that on anyone and if you did then you wouldn't say so out loud, it's just not done. But anyway. Since about eight o'clock this morning the police have been going door to door and we've already been able to weasel out quite a lot of information, give a little take a little, we think, so we like to share what we know, in exchange for the latest details. They're sparing with their information but in any case we now know it was the other woman, not Melodie but the other one, her sister, what's her name, Elsbeth or something, but anyway the one who always looked like she was on the verge of collapse. And now the police want the facts.

The facts. The boys and girls of the CID ask for our understanding; in order not to influence the investigation they can't tell us much about the case, but they can't forbid us from saying what we think. So we simply say they didn't eat, not enough at least, all four of them. Though you ask yourself why so many police, because not eating much isn't illegal as far as we know. We live in a free country. Not that we don't have our opinions on the matter, but everyone leads their own life, don't they? Of course it's going quite far to eat so little that you die. It sets you thinking, when you see what has happened. You can't get it out of your mind. You suddenly see people you didn't have anything to do with in another light when you look back.

They were a strange group of people, anyhow. You don't see it often, four adults sharing a house and doing everything together. You've got couples, you've got families, you've got single people, more and more of those, it's getting more common, even though they probably didn't choose to stay single, alone is alone at the end of the day. But four adults living together? And they were together pretty much all the time. You'd see them walk around here like they were one person. The woman, Melodie, leading the way and the rest following.

Those of us who moved here when the area was still being built remember her from before, when she was in a relationship. A lesbian relationship, it's true, and that was quite unusual at the time, you didn't see it that often back then, but these days all kinds of relationships have become quite the norm. We wouldn't think of it ourselves, not with someone of our own sex, there's still something a bit unnatural about it if you think about it intuitively, but we live in a free country, or did we already say that? Whatever, it seems Melodie's girlfriend left and she married a man after that because she wanted a family like everyone else. Which is understandable. Got cancer at quite a young age, though, so she never saw those kids grow up. It's a tragedy. Waste of time then, in retrospect, that lesbian relationship. But well, it's years ago now. The woman, that Melodie, lived alone for a long time after that. She didn't leave the house much. Our kids called her "the witch" sometimes. A joke of course, an innocent childish joke. There was something witchy about her though, so we could see why. Playing ding-dong ditch with the witch, they liked to do that back then. The mums wondered sometimes whether they should allow it, but well, they were only kids.

Of course it's wasn't nice that her girlfriend had dumped her. But we had the idea that maybe Melodie got bogged down in all that. She didn't do much, to get back out of the dumps. So, well, in that sense we were happy for her when the other three moved in. Which must have been a decade ago, by the way. Time flies, as evidenced. One day three people turned up: one woman her own age, her sister it turned out later, and you could see that, and two younger people, a man and a woman. What they were doing with that woman was a mystery. A young couple, at least that's what we'd assumed at first, that they were a couple, even though we weren't so sure later, but well, in any case two people in the prime of their lives, deciding to live with those two weirdos. No idea what they were doing there, but well, it's not our life.

The other woman, the sister, Elsbeth, we understood. They say she'd had a nervous breakdown and that's why Melodie had taken her in. She looked that way too, as though she was exhausted. And what's better than a family member who takes you in? But why those other two came too, that young couple, even though you never saw them touch, but in any case, those two, what they were doing in that woman's home, no idea.

Weirdos, they were. They did join in with stuff though. Living-room concerts, potluck dinners. Some of us have been into their house. The four of them would sing songs they'd made up themselves. Whether they were any good? Hmm. Each to his own, we always say. It was well meant, they genuinely did their best. They had the best intentions, anyway, we never doubted that. They had admirable ideals. She did, in any case, Melodie. It was always about doing things *together*: working together, living together, sharing things. They weren't cynical, which is admirable when you consider the way things are going with the world. And it seemed relatively harmless. Even though you might think now in retrospect that it was rather worrying. Now the police are crawling all over the place. There were things you could laugh about, but there were also things more likely to make you cry. That man for example, the way he sometimes stood screaming in the back garden, in the middle of the night. Then you'd wonder whether it was all quite healthy and how those four were treating each other. But, well. What can you do? You witness it from a distance and really it's got nothing to do with you, which doesn't give you the right to an opinion. And as long as people aren't murdering each other ...

We hadn't expected this, that something like this would happen. You sometimes think about it, about what can go wrong, particularly with your own children. That someone might suddenly pull a gun or a knife from their inside pocket, or that the man at 47 might be a convicted sex offender who moved here from Amsterdam, or Rotterdam, or some other city with a lot of crime. And you know full well that that woman who lives on the corner didn't walk into a door if you see her sitting at the till with another black eye. Even though this is a respectable neighbourhood apart from that.

They'd got very skinny recently. It was noticeable.

And afterwards you ask yourself whether it wasn't some kind of sect. There was something sect-y about it, some people thought. But that's just speculation. And what is a sect for that matter. They didn't walk along the street singing Hare Krishna. They were quite hippy-dippy but you see that a lot these days. Only that not-eating got to be quite a thing at a certain point. They took it much too seriously, if you ask us. They really believed in it, it seemed, in any case that Melodie did. She was full of conviction when she talked about it, if you ran into her on the street. And those three emaciated housemates of hers who stood there nodding along obediently. Really strange, if you think back. They talked about spiritual liberation, but looking at their faces it was more like spiritual punishment. Hmm, well each to his own is what we thought. Up to a point of course, until it becomes dangerous. But how can you know when it's going to get dangerous? Because now with the police and all those questions being asked you start to wonder whether you shouldn't have intervened. Whether you shouldn't have called someone. Social workers, if they still exist. Or the police. Only you don't want to get involved in things that aren't your business. You see things, you hear things, but is it enough? Those four on the street, moving like a single being. Him, the man, screaming. But how often did that happen, all in all? And what are you supposed to say to social services? That those people aren't eating enough and something must be done?

Sometimes it was like they were from another planet. The way they looked, too. Brightly coloured clothes flapping about their skinny bodies, pallid faces peering out the top. Really different. In principle there's nothing wrong with that, naturally; there's no accounting for taste. If four people want to live together in one house. If that makes them happy. Though we wouldn't want it for ourselves. It's nice to run your own household. Do the washing up whenever you want, keep things neat and tidy, or less tidy, whatever you like, it's up to you, but it's nice to be able to decide that for yourself, in your own family. We think. But well, if they want to live together, the four of them, it's not forbidden. And if they don't want to eat enough, that's allowed. So, yeah. Who knows what they got up to in there. The police can investigate that, it's none of our business. We aren't here to judge our neighbours.

What you do start to think is that you don't know much about the other three. Not about Elsbeth, and not about that couple either. Yes, that man, you heard him screaming sometimes, but Elsbeth and that other woman rarely spoke, almost never. The other one, the younger woman, did smile sweetly when you ran into her. A little apologetically it seemed. Beautiful big eyes she had, even when she started losing weight. There was something energetic about her, but also something frenetic. It didn't look like she was being forced to do anything, it wasn't that. But, well, if you're a Jehovah's witness you don't always feel like you're trapped, that's if you believe the people who've got out.

So yeah, it does raise questions, that's for sure. Whether that Melodie might be less innocent than you'd guess. Whether they didn't have a torture basement or something. But that doesn't seem likely. The houses in that row don't have basements, as far as we know. And she was always going on about butterflies, that Melodie, and about working together, that kind of thing. Very odd, but also innocent in a kind of way. You can't picture her with a knife, absolutely not. That would be more likely to be the man, maybe he was a bit fisty. Maybe he couldn't keep his hands off that girl with the big eyes. Stuff like that. But, well, that's what the police are for. We can't see what goes on behind closed doors. Fortunately not, you might say. Life is already complicated enough. And in the end everyone just has to make the best of it. We live in a free country.

5

We are the counsel. Lawyer, most people would say, but in our job we speak the language of law—a precise language effectively bypassing misunderstandings that could lead to juristic confusion. This is why we are attached to the word "counsel," because it describes our role so precisely, at least in this phase of the criminal investigation.

The criminal investigation: a woman died under suspicious circumstances, probably of malnutrition, with possible culpable negligence by those close to her—her sister and the two other suspects who shared a house with the victim. The suspects were seen by mental health services in connection with confused, over-emotional behaviour and probable psycho-social problems, and although no concrete diagnoses could be made by the health workers, the suspects have been classified as vulnerable. The sister of the victim in particular is very emotional, which is understandable given the family connection, and it is our luck to have been assigned this very client, with whom we are sitting in an interview-slash-interrogation room at the police station for a preliminary meeting, to get acquainted and discuss strategy.

First impression of the client: unhealthily thin,

overcome by emotion, very talkative. Fortunately this is our specialism, seeing through the confusion to distil the information necessary to settle the case as favourably as possible for vulnerable clients. And although *in ultimo casu*, it is not our task to speak the language of the *populus*, we are duly aware that in this phase of the investigation the human aspect of extending support is ninety-nine percent of our work, while the legal aspect only requires one percent of our attention. Priority number one is to put the client at ease. First of all by not looking too imposing in this phase of the investigation: not too much make-up, no smart jackets or high heels, just a blouse, a nice pair of trousers, and smart sneakers. Be approachable. Warm and present in the here and now. Present in heart as well as mind. Listen deeply. Maintain an open attitude, legs straight not crossed, feet on the floor, arms in a relaxed position on the table. A neutral, empathetic facial expression.

Client Mrs Van Hellingen sits facing us with drooping, slightly hunched shoulders. Her hands tremble slightly. She talks about her housemates, she wants to speak to them as soon as possible.

"I see that you are very shocked, is that right?" Show empathy to create a personal connection. "My name is Rose. Would you mind if I called you Melodie, Melodie? I think using first names makes talking easier, don't you?" Address them by their first name to give clients the feeling they are seen, as fellow human beings.

Client Melodie tilts her chin and nods. "It's a nightmare. A real nightmare. Unbelievable that they'd do this to us. My sister dies, after so many years of me trying to help her, then they put me, then they put us, in a prison cell. So inhuman. Don't listen, just rush on. Hiding behind rules and standard procedures. What a terrible system. A terrible, cold system." She shudders. "As though we're dogs not people."

Check the basic conditions of the arrest. "Has anything unconscionable happened to you during your arrest or your time here?"

A look of non-comprehension.

"I mean, can you tell me exactly what happened, Melodie?"

Client takes a deep breath and begins to rattle away like a woman possessed. Hang on, don't judge, keep an open mind and take emotions into account. She's in shock and has a lot to process. Distil the facts about the procedure from emotional consciousness. Suspect arrested on suspicion of culpable homicide due to withholding help at a time of mortal peril, appropriately cautioned by CID, and upon arrival at police station all procedures correctly followed. Reason for detention is sister's death, which the acting GP was unable to put down to natural causes, thus the local coroner and police informed. Client is confused about the concept "natural causes"; keeps repeating that her sister's death was in fact "very natural" and that she and her housemates—client mainly speaks in first-person plural—lead a very natural life and that what is happening now, that she is being prevented from seeing her deceased sister, and is suspected of having killed her, is unnatural. Conceptual confusion in client ignored for time being. Asked what the reason was the doctor couldn't assume natural causes. Main suspicious circumstance seems to be the fact that the victim, but also client and other two suspects are all very underweight and that he didn't like the atmosphere in the house.

Note down relevant facts while maintaining regular eye contact. Client repeats she can't believe that this has happened to them. Her eyes are teary.

"I can see that it has really affected you."

"And not just me. I've had a hellish night, but also because of my housemates. We're used to being together all the time. They are very vulnerable. Petrus suffers from terrible anger issues and if I'm not there to help him channel his blockages he can really get stuck. And Muriel is so impressionable. Who knows what it will do to her if people tell her that Elisabeth's death is our fault. What if she starts to think it's true? And she's extremely sensitive too. With the heavy energy we're being exposed to here, I worry her system will become overloaded. And I kept telling the man with the breakfast that we don't eat artificial, non-organic products, like that bread he brought, and that we're used to surviving on very little food, though Muriel is still strongly attached to her vegetable juice, she hasn't been able to give it up yet. The man didn't understand at all, he was quite rude. He said it wasn't a hotel. Can't you just pop to the organic store, I asked, it's really close by, and they have the right kind of organic carrot juice. But he said it really wasn't possible, and I've no idea how Muriel's going to respond to that. And when I tried to explain how important it is for her, that it's a basic need that you actually can't withhold from a person, even though we are suddenly prisoners, and that if it wasn't possible then it might be a good idea if I went to talk to her to check how she's doing, he cut me off and said that this wasn't possible either, unfortunately, and that I should discuss my complaints with my lawyer, and after that he closed the door, while I was in the middle of a sentence, and—"

Nod understandingly and sneakily check the time. Keep an eye on the goal of the conversation. Lay a hand on the client's wrist and say, "Melodie, I'm sorry I have to interrupt you." Tell them the bad news then explain the situation in layman's terms. "The bad news is that unfortunately according to law you're not allowed to talk to the other suspects, your housemates. This is because the police suspect you all of a crime. To be able to investigate properly what has happened, it's important for them that the three of you are able to tell your own versions of events."

"But we're a collective, a commune. Our stories are all the same. We've been living together for so long. Our own version of events is *our* story, we—"

Be empathetic and persist. "I understand completely that this is your experience of things. And if you all have the same experience then you will all tell the same story. But the police don't know that yet. They want to investigate it. And as you've already heard, they are allowed to keep you here at the police station for the next two days, in any case. So that means you won't be able to speak to each other during that time."

"Two days," client becomes emotional again. "Two

days. But we're a collective. We're not four separate people. We belong together. Muriel and Petrus need me." She stares into space for a moment, as if reflecting. "And after those two days. What then?"

Offer hope but stick to the facts. "It depends on the results of the investigation. There could be reasons to get permission to keep you detained for longer, if it's important for the investigation. But looking at your case, I don't expect this to happen. Eighty percent chance that you can all go home together in three days' time."

"What about my sister? Can we bury her then?"

"Nine times out of ten, the body is released after forensic research. So yes, Melodie, there's a big chance that you will be able to bury your sister—Elisabeth, isn't it? Unfortunately I can't make any promises, but that's my estimation of the case right now."

"This is so unfair," says client shaking her head. "Me, her sister. While I've always helped her so much. She was so vulnerable, so weak. To be honest, she was never the same after her breakdown. And our dad, our dad was so hard on her, so hard. You wouldn't believe it. The last time she called him he just hung up. She really needed our support, the three of us, but especially mine. I mean, the others have come along enormously since they moved in with me, but in the end I was the one who had to carry the burden. And they think that I, that we ..."

We subtly check the time again.

"... and now I'm all on my own," says client as tears stream down her cheeks. "I'm alone. What am I going to do now?"

Client looks at us, fearful, desperate, and suddenly we are overwhelmed by an irrepressible feeling of pity for this woman, chirping for her mother like a tiny wrinkled baby bird with its neck stuck out, and her mother isn't there, but we are, and without reflecting on whether it is appropriate in this professional context, we lay our hand on the client's head and begin to stroke her. "Hush, Melodie, hush now. It will be alright. I'm going to help you, that's why I'm here. I'm here to help you. Hush now. It will be alright, I promise."

Melodie lifts her chin again. "Do you really think so? Really?"

We move our hand to her shoulder and upper arm. All bones, no flesh. "I promise you I'll do everything I can. I'm a good lawyer."

"Can you make sure they let me talk to Muriel then?"

"No, I'm afraid not. We have to stick to the rules. But what I can do is make sure everything runs as smoothly as possible within the rules. So that's what we'll aim for, okay?"

Melodie, client, frowns and takes a deep breath.

"Well done, Melodie, well done. Take a deep breath. We're going to pay close attention so that we are clear about what we're are going to do to get through this as best we can. Alright? It's the best thing you can do for yourself, but also for your housemates. It's best for them too if we think about this carefully. We can't change the fact that you are here now, but we can do everything we can to makes sure you can see your housemates in two days and bury Elisabeth together. So. We've got another quarter of an hour to discuss the case. What do you think? Shall we do that?"

Client sniffs.

"Is that alright, Melodie?"

"Alright," says client. And from this point the professional in us takes over again, with ninety-nine percent of attention for the human side and one crucial percent for the legal angle.

6

We are the facts. Whether we are punishable or not, the best way to approach us is through the lies. Eliminate all the falsehoods until we are naked and revealed. A strong aversion to lies can drive this, as we see with Liesbeth, the detective leading the investigation into the death of Elisabeth van Hellingen. Now she's sitting at the computer with her teeth clenched, struck by the mendacity of the people who preached the gospel that the inhabitants of the Sound & Love Commune have been following for the past few years. They are all very inspiring people who have helped the group enormously in their development, Melodie writes on the commune's website. And with growing indignation, Liesbeth reads an article about one of these people: a woman, a kind of guru, who has written a popular book about "living on light," claiming that she is capable of surviving without food or drink and that anyone can do this by connecting with the Universal Life Force; and though she might not need food she does eat a few crackers sometimes, or has a lick of an ice cream, just for the taste, and now she's saying she doesn't recommend anyone stop eating without support but that her thirty-day plan is suitable for anyone who is sufficiently motivated and truly believes in it. Not only does this woman play fast and loose with us, but she also does so in a very sophisticated way, because whenever anyone challenges her lies, she points to the factual claims she made, alongside all of her lies. She can say she never claimed that she never eats or drinks, only that she doesn't need food and drink to survive. Given she's never stopped eating and drinking for longer than a week, she can't in fact draw this conclusion, though strictly speaking, neither has it been proven that she would have died if she'd kept it up for longer. Proof wasn't even provided when she was subjected to an experiment for a live TV show which followed her as she stopped eating and drinking, because after a couple of days her kidney function was so poor the supervising doctors decided to call a halt to the experiment so that she didn't die, but if she actually would have is still uncertain, so that afterwards the woman was able to say that the experiment had been wrongfully stopped to prevent her from proving that it really was possible to survive on light.

Other women who stopped eating did die, like the woman aptly named Faith, who was found dead in the Scottish Highlands on a solo camping trip. She'd written in her diary that she'd begun the thirty-day fasting process described in the living-on-light guru's book. The autopsy indicated that she'd died of dehydration and hypothermia, but malnutrition was a catalysing factor. And a woman called Ronda had followed the thirty-day programme, supervised by two enthusiastic readers of the book. On the tenth day, Ronda died of pneumonia, kidney failure, dehydration, and a stroke. But does this make it a fact that the book's author would also die if she fasted for long enough? It can't be proved. Clever of her.

We facts know the answer though, because we encompass all of time and space, including all the cause-and-effect relationships in the universe, which is why we can reveal to you here that she *would* die if she tried. Indeed, she will die a few years from now of a medical condition related to nutritional deprivation, but you'd better not tell anyone else, because the world order would be destabilised if people on a large scale knew about the future. Beautiful, if factually incorrect, stories have been written about this.

But the thirty-day woman is not the only person to have pulled the wool over the eyes of the Sound & Love Commune. Maruko and Alina, two young people who must have copied the art from her, are equally inventive with us. They too claim that they don't need food, but it doesn't say anywhere that they never eat. Anyone paying close attention will gather that this couple, parents of healthy boys and girls, do actually eat, only less often. They were also clever enough to reduce the thirty days to nine. In any case this seems more palatable—excuse the pun—for the Sound & Love Commune because Melodie wrote on their website that she had taken the step towards liberation from food under the inspiring guidance of Maruko.

All in all, we are dealt with rather carelessly in no-food-land, and so it's good if there are people who dedicate themselves to us in order to keep others on their toes, people like Liesbeth.

Liesbeth, christened Elisabeth, by total coincidence a namesake of the victim whose death she is investigating, has been given the social task of finding out whether we are punishable, and if so, to deliver proof for this that meets legal requirements. Swearing out loud, she sits at her computer, cursing everyone who isn't very particular about us.

"Jesus," she says, "Jesus Christ. Two deaths on her conscience and she still keeps claiming she doesn't need food. What a crook. She, in any case, should be locked up. And banned from public speaking."

And just like a couple of hours earlier, her colleague Ton, working at the desk diagonally opposite hers, responds that this isn't like Liz, to be so angry, so judgemental, but we can explain her behaviour from a couple of facts that Ton isn't aware of, namely that Liesbeth's daughter Nina has started dieting over the past few months—first losing her puppy fat, then becoming thin, and finally unhealthily skinny—and that she's been refusing to eat meat or cheese for the past couple of weeks. Out of principle, she says, but in the meantime she also leaves most of her rice and pasta, claiming too many fast carbs make her feel dizzy, and Liesbeth, who always wanted to raise her daughter in an atmosphere of acceptance and trust to the point that she'd never have dreamed of poking around in Nina's stuff, found her concerns for her daughter getting the better of her two days ago and so went into her bedroom when Nina was at school, in which she found a strip of laxative pills between the back leg of Nina's bed and the wall, plus a letter addressed to her: *If you read this note, I'll murder you. I'll do what I want anyway. And you won't find my diary so fuck off.*

She found the diary taped to the underside of the second to bottom shelf of Nina's wardrobe and inferred the following from it: Nina had been dieting for four months, and for about eight weeks she'd been doing extensive sets of Fit Girl exercises each day. She'd sought advice to speed up her weight loss on the Pro Ana website, or websites, which had tips for anorexic girls. Nina had copied out and underlined one tip: *Write down what you eat. If you write down what you eat as honestly as possible, you'll stop eating after a while, otherwise it will be in your notebook!* That was where the list of the amounts of food ingested began, carefully noted, down to the gram— Nina had secretly weighed all the things she ate with a set of letter scales to find out exactly how much a teaspoon or tablespoon weighed. With the amount of calories the food contained also noted, Liesbeth could calculate that Nina was only getting about 500 calories a day, and was forced to conclude that her daughter's life was in danger. And this fact, that Liesbeth was seeing her daughter disappear before her eyes, combined with the photos she'd found of an increasingly emaciated Elisabeth with her equally emaciated housemates, and the way in which those same housemates heaped praise on the not-quite-lying Alina and Maruko on their website, made her furious. Which didn't make her the most suitable person to lead the investigation, but like her daughter, Liesbeth is not a person to give up easily once she's sunk her teeth into something, and she tells herself she is quite capable of keeping these

matters separate, because they are essentially different, because the victim in this case didn't have an
eating disorder. But the indignant part of her brain
has a different opinion and says *not eating is not eating, whatever the reason or cause,* and as far as we're
concerned this reasoning is watertight, but the next
thought she has, that people who compel others by
way of lies to starve should be punished, we cannot
as facts confirm or deny; to our regret we must leave
moral judgements up to others. For Liesbeth too it
would be more sensible to solely focus on us, but we
don't actually have much of a say in that.

Shaking her head, Liesbeth gets up, picks up her
notebook and walks away from her computer. She
has an appointment with Asif, a new colleague who
is going to interview the suspects with her. He is
still a young man but is just as driven as Liesbeth in
his own way. A couple of years ago he retrained after
working as an economist, because he wanted to do
something more meaningful for society. His thesis
was about interviewing vulnerable suspects and
now he has been designated the team's specialist in
that area.

"Coffee?" he asks as she goes into the meeting
room where he is waiting. He frowns. "Are you alright?"

"Fine, thanks. And I don't need a coffee. Let's just
dive right in."

Asif nods and begins to hold forth on vulnerable
suspects: what vulnerable suspects need in general,
what he has found out so far about the background
of these suspects, and what this means in terms of
the best way to approach the examination. Liesbeth

listens in silence, her arms tightly folded and her lips drawn into a straight line.

"My research also showed that body language is very important too, by the way," Asif says. "So, for example, the way you are sitting now. It could come across to vulnerable suspects as rather ... how to put it? It might trigger a feeling of panic." He winks. "Only joking. But seriously, I think it would be better if you adopted a more open posture with them, like this maybe."

He leans forward, rests his hands casually on the table, and pulls up the corners of his mouth slightly.

Liesbeth crosses her legs. "Alright, Asif. It's great that you wrote a thesis, but I have enough practical experience in the job to know how to talk to a suspect. And vulnerable suspects aren't just vulnerable, but also suspects. We mustn't forget that. So given that we only have half an hour left, I suggest that we spend the rest of the time on the facts we want to bring out into the open." She looks at her watch. "Twenty-five minutes because first I'm going to smoke a cigarette. Do you want one? Or is it against your religion?"

"That's rather a discriminatory question, if I may say so. I make my own decisions and I've decided to keep my lungs healthy. You could do that too. Or is it against your religion?"

Liesbeth coughs. "Alright. Sorry, you know, I didn't mean to offend you." She reaches into her pocket for a lighter. "You're right though. Very sensible. I'll be right back."

And still boiling with rage about people who, encouraged by charlatans and liars, wilfully seek out death, she takes the lift to the roof terrace, where she chain-smokes two cigarettes.

7

We are the scent of oranges. Since the detective who goes by the name Asif entered the interview room, we've been unmistakeably present to anyone with a good sense of smell. And Petrus has a good sense of smell, particularly where the scent of oranges is concerned. As fleeting and invisible as we are, we effortlessly get into people's minds, releasing in a flash memories and feelings which they'd hoped were forgotten, and as soon as we reach the receptors in Petrus's nose he becomes filled with rage. The rage comes from deep within, from long ago, but the images we arouse in him are almost tangible. The lips of a boy with blond spiky hair and a face covered in acne, who soundlessly mouths the words "stinky-orange wimp," strands of saliva stretching from his tongue to the roof of his mouth. A bag, a red rucksack from an expensive brand. A row of bared yellow, coffee-stained teeth topped by a grey moustache. And his mother's face, in which irremediable disappointment can be read.

The rucksack was new. It was a nice bag in a lovely red, and Petrus had pestered his mother, who thought it much too expensive, until she'd given in. It was the first day he'd taken it to school and, since he didn't trust his classmates, he hadn't taken his eyes off it for a second. During the lunch break he'd put it in his locker, though, so he could go to the toilet, because bags weren't allowed in the loos.

But when he went to get out his biology book after lunch, we suddenly appeared, seemingly from nowhere—though in reality from the bottom of his bag—and entered his nose, along with a stale mouldy smell. Petrus felt his face pull tight. He slowly put his biology book on the table. Its pale blue cover had turned green at the bottom, as had the cover of his maths text book, when he pulled that out, and his economics book, and his exercise books.

There were two mouldy oranges at the bottom of his new bag.

Petrus stared at the oranges, thinking about what his form tutor had told him. "I've warned them, but if anything does happen again, please count to ten first. Just count to ten. If you get angry, you only reward their efforts."

He reached seven. Then he looked up, right into the eyes of the spiky-haired boy who he'd instantly realized must have done it. The boy looked at him, smiling, and mouthed the words "stinky-orange wimp."

The caretaker, thought Petrus. Without speaking, he left the classroom, the two oranges in his hands, ignoring the biology teacher's calls, and stormed to the caretaker's office.

"Did you give that bastard the master key for the lockers?"

The caretaker held up his hands. "The lockers? I don't know what you're talking about." He let his hands drop. "But I always say, nothing wrong with a joke. That's what I think. Makes school life a little more bearable." And he grins, but two seconds later he stops, because then Ben, voted caretaker of the year in 1984, gets a mouldy orange pressed into each eye.

It was the first time that Petrus found himself in the dock. He'd often been told off for the damage he caused when he lost his cool, but never had the accusations been so serious, or so unfair, he felt. He had to come to school with his mother for a conversation with the headmaster, the chair of the school board, and the caretaker who maintained that he'd been joking, he never would have given the master key to a pupil. Everyone knew that the caretaker was quite sloppy with the rules and that he and the spiky-haired boy were in cahoots, but the headmaster and the chair refused to believe Petrus, as did his mother, and even if the caretaker had lent out the master key, what Petrus had done to him remained unacceptable. It was nothing less than an act of aggression, which the caretaker could have reported to the police, so he could be happy he'd got off with a suspension. He'd had to stay home for two weeks and do domestic chores for his disappointed mother. Afterwards he'd been condemned to the daily use of a bag in which we were always vaguely present, because he couldn't subject his mother to no longer wanting the bag along with everything else.

Since then he hasn't been able to smell us without getting angry, especially when he's not expecting us, and because he's nervous about being questioned, and he wants to do everything he can not to lose his temper, he folds his arms and keeps his eyes fixed downward.

Asif takes a deep breath. As he eats an orange after lunch every day, he hardly notices us, but he recognizes Petrus's body language as a textbook example of a vulnerable suspect. Make space, don't pressurise, that's the key, he thinks. To put the suspect at ease, he leans back and slowly moves his hand to his coffee mug to take a sip, not realizing that by moving the hand he just used to peel the orange, he is only making the smell situation worse. Again, we emphatically penetrate Petrus's nose, and a new wave of anger rises up in him that could go one of two ways: either he'll burst or he'll turn inwards. He turns inwards. Anger settles in his neck muscles and his face. But he doesn't manage to keep it all inside and certainly not now he has to answer the question Asif asks him at the same time: "Tell me about yourself." His throat is closed, his mouth is closed, his head, everything is closed. Petrus clutches his folded arms even more tightly to himself. He looks down, he looks up at the ceiling, he looks to one side, to his lawyer, but he doesn't manage to utter a single word. He is trapped inside his body.

Asif frowns. "Does he want to invoke the right to remain silent?" he asks Petrus's lawyer, a robust woman with cropped grey hair, wearing a dark suit. "Or do you need a little more time?" And he suggests taking a break so that Petrus and his lawyer can discuss what the matter is.

Liesbeth and Asif leave the room, leaving us behind in almost imperceptible quantities.

"Sir," says the lawyer. "Mr Zwarts, what's happening? What's the matter with you? It's important you try to answer the questions."

His jaw muscles clench.

"You're upset," she says. "Will you tell me why you're upset?"

A brief shake of the head.

"Are you afraid?"

Again, no.

"Is it something we need to discuss?"

No.

"Do you think you'll be able to calm down?"

He takes a big breath.

"Would it help to sigh?" the lawyer suggests.

He sighs a few times.

"That's the ticket," she says.

Petrus thinks of Melodie. He tries to remember what she used to say at times like this. Feel your feeling. Find the connection. Breathe through your resistance. He breathes through his resistance. And suddenly he thinks of a cigarette, which isn't because of us but the hint of cigarette smoke that Liesbeth has left in the room, and he asks whether he might have a cigarette. Would that be allowed? A quick smoke? But his lawyer says it's really not possible, they only have a couple of minutes' consulting time, they're in the middle of the examination, and the detectives could return any moment.

"Do you think you'll manage? Try to breath calmly? I'm here with you. Should I repeat what I just explained? They'll probably ask questions about your life and you can just answer them truthfully. And the same goes for questions about last night. If you're unsure, you can always ask to consult with me. I'm here and I'll intervene immediately if anything happens that isn't in your best interests. Alright?"

Petrus says alright and the detectives come back, and in the meantime the last traces of orange have almost disappeared from Asif's hands, fortunately, so that our presence remains sufficiently subtle to no longer make Petrus white-hot with rage; and with Asif and Liesbeth's questions about his daily life, the cloud of memories of his school days are replaced by a different cloud, without men and boys, but with women, three women, two mature and one young. The detectives want to know how he met these women and why he moved in with them; why did he decide to do that? Petrus breathes in and out, his mind searches the cloud, trying to formulate an answer.

Why did he move in with them? He doesn't know. It just happened. He'd been fired again after yet another fight and he'd decided to go into therapy to learn to manage his anger. In the library he'd found a leaflet about a kind of therapy based on feelings and music. Since he didn't like talking much but did enjoy listening to music, he'd thought that might suit him and so he'd made an appointment with Melodie. The first sessions were short but they'd gradually grown longer, sometimes they'd spent hours talking and doing exercises. Then there were group sessions with others of Melodie's clients, sessions that sometimes took days, but that didn't matter because he had the time. And then Melodie had suggested taking a whole week. All going away together for a whole week, to a large house in the woods near Nunspeet, to explore their relationship with each other.

They'd run the gamut of all possible emotions that week. They'd shouted, cried, laughed, and sometimes cautiously touched when Melodie had said they could hold hands. They'd all smiled then, and all agreed that this was a lovely moment, a moment of connection. After a week, or maybe it was two, he can't remember it that clearly, the holiday was over, and after they'd all packed and were about to leave, Melodie had called everyone together. They sat in a circle on the lawn behind the house, their luggage piled in a heap, as Melodie said her piece. She said she thought there was more in this, that it had potential, that everyone could dive deep and soar high if they continued with this for longer, if they made it their way of life, and that's why she'd decided to open her house up for anyone who was interested. Anyone who wanted could come and live with her and they'd continue along this path together.

A long silence followed. Some people looked away, others asked questions. How many people can fit in your house? Who's going to earn our keep? Where are we supposed to sleep? Melodie said, "We'll figure that all out. Anyone who wants to join, is in. If the house turns out to be too small, we'll look for a bigger place. If problems occur, we can address them together until we all agree with each other. Anyone who doesn't want to join can leave the circle now and go. Our friendship won't be affected, I promise. But maybe it would be an idea to take home the question: what are you actually running away from? And how long you want to keep on running?"

Petrus didn't want to keep on running. He didn't want to be a person who runs away. I'm not a fleer, he thought, I'm a fighter. So he stayed. For a moment he thought he'd be the only one, but once almost everyone had left the circle, he saw that Muriel had remained seated too. And as though it were the most natural thing in the world, they'd picked up their bags and gone home with Melodie.

In the beginning it seemed like a continuation of the holiday. Melodie had suggested they sleep on their airbeds the same way, side by side in the sitting room. They went to bed together, got up together. They spent the day together. Like him, Muriel didn't have a job, or she did have one but she'd called in long-term sick, so they had plenty of time. After a week Petrus went back to his old house to pick up some stuff. He gave notice on his rental contract and the day he handed back the keys he put the rest of his belongings out with the trash.

"Great," Melodie had said. "Great you managed to let go of your old life so easily. You'll have got rid of a lot of ballast with those belongings. So that's that gone."

They didn't do much besides eat, sleep, sing, and talk. Lots of talk. Mainly Muriel who drove the others to distraction with her talking.

A week after the three of them had set up home together, Elisabeth had joined them. Silently, almost unnoticed, she'd added herself to the group. She spoke even less than he did. He and Elisabeth were the quiet ones.

"You shut yourself off," Melodie said when she felt they didn't talk enough. "You avoid contact."

Avoiding contact was wrong. And to help them to stay connected, Melodie would write them lines in crayon on little pieces of paper, which they could say to themselves. *I am connected to the whole world. The other is a mirror of my deepest self. I can open my heart to everybody.*

"Petrus?" says Asif. "Did you hear the question? Why did you join the group? Can you tell us something about that?"

Petrus looks up. "For personal development. So I could get better at connecting. To learn how to cope with my blockages."

The detectives enquire further and Petrus does his best to give the right answers. He hears himself talking, words that seem to come from Melodie's mouth, and he thinks he believes them, but at the same time he's not exactly sure what they mean.

Elisabeth isn't mentioned until right at the end. Elisabeth, who really wasn't good at connecting. Who barely dared to move, and never took the initiative to speak. Who took up so little space that they often forgot she was there. Only when she sat colouring with her crayons did he sometimes spot a small smile on her face.

"Nice, Elisabeth," Melodie would say then. "Let it in. It's allowed, feeling nice."

Elisabeth was a kind of pet to Melodie, a human being who lived and breathed as they all did, but to whom they couldn't talk on the same level, Petrus thinks to himself. But he stays superficial with his questioners. He says she found it hard to connect, she was often very quiet but he did get the impression that life in the commune did her good.

"And your diet? Can you explain a bit about it?"

"Diet?"

"Is it true that you'd all stopped eating?" Liesbeth wants to know.

And again he replies with words that aren't his own. Letting go of food, living a purer life, not taking any more than you actually needed.

"Can you tell us anything about yesterday evening when Elisabeth became ill?"

He reluctantly tells them about it.

"Did you think to call a doctor at all?"

"We didn't think it was necessary."

"Who didn't think it was necessary?"

"Melodie was with her."

"Did you discuss the possibility?"

"What possibility?"

"The possibility of calling a doctor."

"No."

"And you didn't think of it yourself?"

"No."

"Did you think she might die?"

"I didn't think so, no."

"So you thought she'd survive this."

"No, I didn't think that either."

"What did you think then?"

Petrus reflects. "Nothing," he says.

Liesbeth straightens her back. "Your housemate lies dying before your eyes and you think of nothing?"

Asif glances to the side and makes a conciliatory gesture and for a moment we're worried this will set off a new fit of rage in Petrus, but Petrus can no longer smell us. He's tired. Tired of talking about things he doesn't want to talk about.

"I was trying to be present," he says. "In the moment."

Liesbeth exchanges a glance with Asif and looks at her watch, and without knowing it, she brings another smell into the air, and into Petrus's consciousness—that of cigarette smoke.

He looks at his lawyer. "I want a cigarette. I want to stop and I want a cigarette. And I'm invoking my right to silence until I've smoked one."

8

We are Sound and Love. We probably would never have chosen each other but since we've been displayed on a nameplate together next to Melodie's front door, linked by an ampersand, we've grown to appreciate one another. We've grown fond of each other, Love would say, but Sound thinks more in terms of resonance, which according to him shows that we don't always have to be on the same wavelength, but that in spite of this, we get along pretty well together. A deep affection can develop even in an arranged marriage, Love thinks, while Sound echoes that he sees it more as an unexpected harmony.

"I want something that captures our essence," Melodie had said. She was sitting with her new housemates on the living-room floor. "Something that's important to all of us, that will inspire all of us. I thought of Love myself, because that's what it's all about in the end with us, don't you think? Love for ourselves, for each other, and for the world. And to experience more fully how those three things are actually the same at a deeper level." She looked at her housemates. "What do you think?"

Muriel nodded. "Nice, yes. The Love Commune. Or

just Love? Or Commune of Love? Or house. House of Love."

She sought the eyes of the other two. Petrus's face was illegible, Elisabeth was frowning at her hands.

"Great," said Melodie. "Very good that you're thinking along with me, Muriel. Nice that you are contributing. We've all got a voice in this commune and we must all be heard. So it's good that you are making use of this opportunity." She closed her eyes, breathed slowly and audibly in and out and looked around the circle again. "Yes. So Love, we agree with that. And another thing important to me, to us, is music. Harmony. Sound. Sound is such a powerful means of connecting with each other. To truly feel the energy of our love. You've experienced that too, of course."

"That's nice too, yes," said Muriel. "Love and Sound Commune."

"Yes," agreed Melodie. "Yes, I get you saying it that way, because naturally Love is the most important, in a certain way. Love is closer to the goal and Sound the medium. But I'd thought of putting them the other way round, because of the cadence. I'm quite sensitive to that. So Sound and Love Commune. What do you think? Petrus? Elisabeth?"

And so we were united in the name of Melodie's new commune, just like that, on a rainy Tuesday afternoon. And later when Love cautiously asked Sound whether he hadn't found it painful to be set aside as the less important one, Sound replied that in the end he had been placed first, with the argument that the name as a whole sounded better like that, so that Love might be more important in theory but Sound had tipped the scales in practice, a pattern that we often saw repeated in the early years of our commune. In theory, Sound was the means to Love, but in practice, Love sometimes needed to be put aside when it came to setting the right tone.

Melodie had suggested making music together to feed their love for each other. And they wanted to perform together to spread this love to the world.

"In the future it could be a way for us to earn money," she added, something that Love in all her benevolence was prepared to believe, while Sound had his doubts from the start because Muriel couldn't sing in tune. Tone-deaf, Sound concluded with certainty when he heard Muriel sing during their first a cappella session, and Love tried to temper this judgement somewhat, but Sound was not to be budged, explaining that it wasn't a judgement, simply a fact, as far as he was concerned. It was like blindness or dyslexia, he said, a congenital defect, a missing connection in the brain—Sound didn't know the exact cause but the defect was unmistakeable. And however patiently and amicably Melodie kept explaining it, singing it for her, explaining and demonstrating again, and however faithfully Muriel practised, not just during practice sessions but also during all her other free moments, when she was cleaning the kitchen or weeding the garden, her voice just couldn't sing in tune, and Melodie could get quite furious in her frustration about it. Petrus found it hard to stay patient too; he'd hit the right notes immediately and when everything had to be repeated for the nth time for Muriel, it sometimes got too much for him. He'd flee outside to the garden to cool off, or would stamp upstairs, and Melodie would go after him to make the choir complete again. Love is not quick to say negative things about people, but the way Sound heard her sigh, he understood it wasn't easy for her, with all those frictions and arguments, and so to console her Sound would often sing a love song.

After several months of troublesome vocal sessions, Melodie decided to switch to instruments. She bought four lutes and four viola da gambas, which the other three were going to learn to play. It would help them tune in better to themselves and to each other, she said. The strings of the lute wobbled beneath Petrus's sweaty fingers, he couldn't do it and wanted to cast away the instrument. Melodie said, "Breathe through it, breathe through your resistance." And sometimes he would breathe through his resistance, but often he didn't manage in the end and he'd hurl the lute onto the sofa and storm out of the room.

"Doesn't matter," Melodie would say to the other two, who looked at her sheepishly from behind their lutes. "He just has to work through this. He's never learned to deal with failure in an adult manner. It will work out. Let's start again from the first bar."

She continued to tirelessly give her housemates music lessons, and have conversations about feelings, because this was another important activity of life in the commune. Nothing you felt was ever wrong, Melodie claimed. Feelings were always good and instructive, even if there was screaming or crying or slammed doors, because only by feeling and sharing your emotions did you genuinely connect, and so each argument brought them a step closer to each other. The fact they'd committed to each other and the group unconditionally provided a sense of security. "It means you always know you're in it together, and you'll come out of it together, too."

And this was equally true for us, because across the years, the two of us have gone through quite a few difficult periods together. When Sound was at the end of his tether because Melodie insisted on only playing Renaissance music—performed badly on top of it, without a clear rhythm, and with lots of long sustained notes—Love was there with her comforting arms. And Sound was there for Love too, when she'd had to look on in disappointment as Melodie called everyone together because she thought they should all express their feelings, while it was as clear as day that two of them didn't want to. Petrus would say he felt oppressed and coerced, Melodie would respond that this made her feel hurt and ask Petrus how that made him feel, Petrus would then tie himself up in knots because, on one hand, he didn't want to talk about his feelings simply because Melodie was forcing him to, while on the other, he was brimming with rage and had to work really hard to keep a lid on those feelings. He'd stare silently into his glass of herbal tea, especially if Melodie went on to ask Muriel what Petrus's behaviour made *her* feel, and Muriel would reply that Petrus's closedness made her feel quite sad, so that Petrus, after Melodie had asked him how it made him feel that he provoked these feelings in Muriel, would find himself compelled to smash the glass of tea against the wall. When Love had had enough of such interactions, Sound was always quick to distract her with a cheerful musical classic or a forgotten hit from the 1950s, or simply some comforting noises.

And what Love would like to add, before a very negative image of Melodie arises, is that the latter's persistence really is admirable. In her own, perhaps not always effective way, but with endless dedication, Melodie has always stayed faithful to us. Despite Muriel's unmusicality, despite Petrus's rage, despite Elisabeth's silence. And she has managed to do a lot: she succeeded in teaching the other three to harmonise, not entirely in tune but close enough, and to play the lute, and the viola da gamba. Simple pieces, but still. She adjusted her ambitions: to dare to have the group, as imperfect as it was, perform in public. She even succeeded in earning money with music, more or less, at the start, when Muriel, who was good at filling out forms, helped her to apply for a grant, which they then received, for the group to play music together with primary-school children. Sound would never have thought this was possible after the first practice session. And Love did sometimes get her share too, when Melodie and the others sat in the garden on summer's evenings, resting after all the practicing and talking, when there was a little space, then Love could really feel that, through all the confusion, they had grown to love each other—and that could be described as something special. Even though it is a shame it had got so out of hand at the end. That we got so out of balance. Love had misjudged that, the importance of Sound, because secretly Love had thought that her universal power would be enough to keep the world turning. Sound saw things differently, he'd always thought that Love was quite abstract. Not that he didn't consider her important, or that he didn't think she sounded wonderful, such a universal principle, but it's not the kind of thing that helps with concrete decision-making, with figuring out what you're going to do all day, Sound thought. However beautiful you are, Love, you're not enough to survive on alone.

And bit by bit, Love had found herself obliged to agree with Sound. Because when they were able to perform less often, when the financial crisis came along, and there was no new grant for primary-school projects and all four of them had to survive on Elisabeth's welfare benefits, that's when the emptiness began to grate. Their rehearsals tailed off. They still sang every day, but it all became less frequent, less focussed. The urgency had gone. And sometime during that period they gradually became more occupied with food. In the name of so-called Love. But don't go thinking that Love wanted this, which Sound can wholeheartedly back up. And in retrospect that was the beginning of the end, we think. In any case, the end of Elisabeth. If they'd only kept listening to Sound, it wouldn't have all gone wrong, Sound often says to Love, shaking his head. Elisabeth's life might not have struck its final chord so prematurely. And Love nods, a little admiringly, though she'd never say that out loud, because she knows he can't handle compliments, but inside she secretly glows when she hears him speaking so wisely, and she thinks to herself: he hits just the right note, dear Sound. I couldn't have made it sound better myself.

9

We are the parents. The father actually, Elisabeth and Melodie's father, but their mother surely won't mind me speaking for both of us. Leaning upright against the pillow, I sit on my side of the marital bed waiting for the second digit of my alarm clock on my bedside cabinet to jump from five to six, after which I can finally allow myself to get out of bed. That was always our agreement, because Hansje liked to sleep longer, and even though she's sleeping in a different bed now, in a different house, where there are people who can take care of her, I don't want to just break our agreement because she's gone, as though in her going she'd disposed with it entirely. What's more, what would I do with myself, out of bed so early? The paper hasn't arrived yet and it's too early to have breakfast. I wish I could fall back asleep but that's not going to happen, certainly not in this heat. Even with the windows open against each other it hardly cooled down last night.

"Now Mum's gone, you might consider sleeping downstairs," Johan had said after the move. "Then you won't have to go up and down the stairs each time."

A tempting thought, but that would really be betraying Hansje, rearranging the whole house to suit your own preferences and desires the moment she's gone. And on top of that, I don't want to give in to old age before the battle has been fought. As long as I can go up and down the stairs, I'll go up and down the stairs.

But for now, I'm sitting in bed, among the sweaty sheets, attempting to calm down my thoughts about the case. The news that Elisabeth has died and Melodie has been arrested has made me feel dizzy. An important anchor has gone, the certainty that our children, however different they became than we'd hoped, were in any case capable of taking care of themselves, and each other when necessary.

Fortunately the other three have never disappointed us as far as that goes. Particularly Johan. Johan has always been a rock for everyone around him. I don't know what we'd do without him. As soon as Melodie had hung up—she couldn't speak for long, the police were there and she was only allowed to pass on the most important things about her arrest—I called him. It was the middle of the night, but he picked up immediately. Such a reliable, good boy, he is.

"How awful, Dad. Awful. You don't deserve this. We didn't deserve this." He was silent for a moment. "You must be worrying about what to do about the funeral, I expect. We'll find out. But tomorrow, Dad. We'll do that tomorrow. Do you think you'll manage to sleep or should I come to you?"

"No, you don't need to, son. That's quite a trek for you. And you'll lose half a workday tomorrow."

"That doesn't matter. I don't have any meetings tomorrow as it happens, and my sermon for Sunday is just about done."

"Oh good, well, that's nice. But are you sure—?"

"Yes, I'm sure. I'll come."

That kind of son, such a caring son, so dedicated to his work and to us, it would be nice if everyone could have one like that.

He was here within half an hour, and the next day we looked into what to do about the funeral, or rather Johan did, making a couple of calls to an old friend from his fraternity, a bigwig in criminal justice, and another friend in civil rights. The legal details have slipped my mind again, but a lot depended on the matter of whether Melodie would be released before Elisabeth's body, because in that case we would have to ensure that we got permission to bury the body before Melodie did, but if Melodie was detained for longer, we could approach the relevant authorities to arrange the funeral without any bother from her. Melodie wouldn't be able to attend, which would be very painful for her of course, but given the history, it could be best for all concerned.

As parents we've been blamed for the problems with Elisabeth and Melodie in many ways. The things we did wrong according to Melodie, and the good things we failed to do. I could write a book about it. But I don't feel like sharing the nitty-gritty of our old family life with others. It's not necessary either. Leave that to Melodie. It wouldn't surprise me if she blamed us for Elisabeth's death too. Not much surprises me where Melodie is concerned.

But Melodie is still alive. Elisabeth is dead. Strange, how much you can forget about your children. Ask me about Elisabeth's first steps, the first word she spoke, I wouldn't know. Elisabeth was Elisabeth. Quiet, responsible, intelligent. After Johannes, Johan, she was our first girl. But what kind of girl exactly, I no longer know. Even Elisabeth's face, on the family photo which Hansje always had on her nightstand until she moved, I can hardly picture. While I could describe Melodie just like that, with the straight fringe she had then and the way she looked sternly into the camera.

We never had favourites, each of our children was as sweet as the rest, but one child sometimes attracts more attention than the others. And Melodie, our third child, the middle one of the five, had our attention right from the start. She wasn't the cleverest of the children, not at all, but there was something about her, as though she understood things in a different, more adult manner. She had that from a very young age, even before she could talk. She'd sit in her high chair with custard all over her face and look at us as though she was about to ask us a question about the existence of God, or the meaning of original sin. And she was the only one who reacted to the records we played on Sundays when we came back from church. The only one who had a real feel for the beauty of Bach, Mahler, Sibelius, and all our other favourites. She'd listen attentively to the names of the instruments being played. Violin, oboe, cello, flute, cello, cello.

"Seyo. Seyo."

"What's that? Did you say cello?"

"Seyo."

"Cello, she's saying cello!"

"Seyo."

That was her first word. Cello. Truthfully. Only after that did she say dada and mama.

An unusual child she was, and born for music. Not because of her name, even though her mother liked to think so. I'd rather have chosen a more classical name. Clara, for instance, or Alma. But her mother insisted she be called Melodie. She didn't always have the best taste, Hansje, and she was quite impressionable. Her cousin from Canada had called her daughter Melodie and when Hansje read that in one of her letters she became set on calling our third child Melodie if it was a girl, and there was no budging her.

"I'm her mother," she said, "and you already chose Johan and Elisabeth's names." Which wasn't true because we'd simply named them after their paternal grandfather and maternal grandmother, as befitting.

"Who has had to carry that child for the past twenty-three weeks? Who will have to carry it for the next few months? And who will have to give birth to it? And breastfeed it? Not you, right?"

External influences made her talk like that. Her cousin from Canada, who had done teacher training here in the Netherlands and now lived on a remote farm, alleviating her loneliness by reading women's magazines and writing inflammatory letters to Hansje about women's rights and the dangers of modern agricultural methods. Her cousin had read about the latter in a book called *Silent Spring*, which she said was one of the most important books to be published in recent times, and Hansje had bought it immediately, from her housekeeping money, without consulting me first. A depressing book, filled with unfounded claims about the so-called damaging effects of the technology that had been so important to our country during the post-war reconstruction period. But Hansje had lapped it all up and even copied out a quote from the jacket to hang above Melodie's bed. *Filled with love, a human bends over a child's cradle ... and simultaneously allows its food to be poisoned. For how much longer?*

All kinds of ideas she got into her head, Hansje, it wasn't always easy, not with child-rearing either. She was their mother so I wanted to stand by her, not criticise her. But she criticised me though. If I asked why Maarten had scored a six out of ten for maths and not an eight, she'd say a six was good enough. If I urged Melodie to practice her scales more carefully, she said the feeling was more important than hitting the right notes. When I asked why she'd put away my shirts unironed in the wardrobe, she said she'd been reading research about the toxic additions to detergents and a few creases here and there had a certain cheer. And she tried to convince our children of nature's destruction by industry. So in the interest of their education, I did sometimes find myself compelled to provide counterbalance. I'd make a joke about it, to make it clear in a light-hearted way who was right. Furious she'd get, truly furious, especially if the children enjoyed it.

"I won't let myself be pushed into a corner," she'd cry. "I'm not a nobody, a nothing."

"Oh, but a nothing, a zero, is such a lovely number," I'd reply, winking at the children. "If you put on a belt and do it up tight, you can be an eight."

And the children would be on the floor again, laughing. Only Elisabeth seemed more interested in her food, and Melodie would look from me to Hansje and back, and ask whether she could get down from the table to go study.

Hansje. May the Lord have mercy on her soul. Even though she's not dead yet. She's already far gone. There's not much left of her old personality. How easily she agreed to move into a nursing home—"If that's best for everyone, then that's best for everyone," she'd said when I explained it to her—and although she was very upset when we said goodbye to her that first evening, she's been very cooperative for the rest.

If only she'd been more like that earlier. If only she'd listened when I said we shouldn't spoil the children. We shouldn't pat Melodie on the back when she didn't deserve it. If only she'd understood that talent can't blossom fully if children only get compliments and cuddles. Fatherhood would have been a lot easier. I wouldn't have had to bear the responsibility of preparing our children for the future alone. To reward achievements but also to draw attention to failings and to guide the child in the right direction with a firm but gentle hand. To make sure they all did their homework, and that Melodie also did enough cello practice. It wasn't always easy, being the strict parent all the time.

Sometimes I wonder what it would have been like if I'd picked a different wife. A more sober, firmer type of woman. If Melodie and Elisabeth had had a different kind of mother, who showed interest in their father's trials and tribulations. Who'd genuinely been curious about my work, the issues that preoccupied me, the challenges and the triumphs. A woman like Mary-Lou from the town hall, who wanted to know things, who shared my experiences, who understood the importance of a working life.

If I had, those two might not have drifted so far away, they would have learned to stick up for themselves. But Melodie doesn't think the same way, neither on her own or Elisabeth's behalf. She says it's all my fault. I wasn't nice enough to their mother. My jokes about her divergent world view weren't funny, but mean. I was too strict on the kids. I always took our sons more seriously than our daughters. Which isn't true, absolutely not true. If I took anyone seriously, if I gave anyone time and attention, it was Melodie.

It's sad, the way she manoeuvred away from us, taking Elisabeth with her. The last time I heard her voice, Elisabeth's, I hung up without speaking. Not because I didn't want to talk to her but because I didn't believe it was Elisabeth who was talking. It was her voice but the words and sentences were incredibly strange. This was a marionette, a soulless being that recited, or perhaps read aloud, something that someone else had told her to say: that she'd been unable to really connect with us during her youth and that she regretted this but that I could make things up to her by allowing her and her housemates to spend more time with their mother in the nursing home. These weren't Elisabeth's words but Melodie's.

Johan says I shouldn't feel guilty about refusing to speak with Melodie via Elisabeth that evening. "It wouldn't have been a fruitful conversation, Dad. It would have only caused more misery; you judged it well. You did what you could. It's very sad what happened. Very sad for all of us. For Melodie too, but she also has to learn that her behaviour has consequences. So have a good think about what you want to do with the funeral. If you like, Bert can give us some free advice, in case Melodie is allowed home in two days' time. The most important thing is for you to say a proper goodbye to your daughter. You're her father."

Regrettable that it had to happen this way. That we'll probably have to fight one daughter for the other daughter's body. And that Elisabeth has gone for good. If only I'd paid more attention. Her first steps, her first words, her first school report. I really wish I could bring to mind a lovely memory of her. But nothing comes, and the five on the clock still hasn't turned into a six.

10

We are a butterfly. A beautiful, newly hatched butterfly that lives inside Muriel's head. At least once a day, but usually more often, we crawl out of our cocoon and unfold our wings in the sunlight, the patterns on our wings contrasting impressively with a blueish-yellow morning sky. Like a peacock butterfly, we have a round patch on each of our wings that looks like a peacock's feather, but unlike the peacock butterfly, our patches are exactly the same colour as a peacock's feather—dark blue in the middle, with a pale blue ring around it, then a broader, shiny brown band, and finally a circle of green. And around the circles, our wings are a fuchsia pink. If you know about butterflies, you'll know that these patterns don't actually exist, but then we're not a real butterfly, we're a product of Muriel's mind. After we've hatched she usually lets us lie motionlessly in the sunlight for a while so that she can take her time admiring our wings before she has us fly up from the leaf we're sitting on, to the tree-canopied horizon.

This morning is the same. Muriel is kneeling with her eyes closed in front of a slice of bread covered with chocolate sprinkles, wondering whether or not she should eat it. In a moment of weakness, she took the bread from its wrapper and poured the sprinkles onto it. They are already beginning to go nice and soft in the heat, but she's firmly convinced it would be better to leave it untouched and to tell the custody officer that she changed her mind, and this is why she has closed her eyes and is looking at us inside her head, watching us as the sunlight caresses our wings and we fly away in slow motion. We have to inspire her to control herself, and to stick to her resolution to stay empty and light.

The first time Muriel pictured us she was sitting in Melodie's living room in the house she'd later move into, with her legs pulled up under her in a pale yellow armchair as Melodie sat facing her on the red sofa.

"In these sessions I'm mainly going to help you to reach your full potential," Melodie said. "That's the main goal of the therapy. And something I've noticed that can really help is to work with images. Something that can inspire you. That shows you where you want to go in life, as it were. You can decide what that image should look like, but from my own experience I'd recommend picking something from nature. A flower or a butterfly, for example. Because natural things are, for most people, easier to connect with on a deeper level."

Muriel nodded. "Alright, yes. An image. Do I have to choose now?"

"No, wait a while. We'll let the image arise. You don't have to choose, you can just open up to it. See what comes, whether it's a flower, a tree, a butterfly, or something very different. Everything's possible. It's your image. So if you like you can close your eyes now." She waited a moment. "Good, yes. Breathe in and out calmly a few times. And with each exhalation let go of some of your tension. Interference. Background noise. Pressure. And you can take in some light with every inhalation. Some air. Love for yourself."

"Breathe in and out a few times. Alright," said Muriel. "Do you mean two times or three times? Or more?"

"Three, four, five, it's not about numbers. It's about what you feel and experience inside. It's about making yourself empty enough to be able to connect with whatever will make your potential the most clearly visible."

Muriel nodded and decided that another five breaths would be the best; the more exhalations the emptier, she thought, and the emptier the better, but she was only at her third inhalation when Melodie began to speak again.

"Great," she said, "and now that you're a little more relaxed and present, start to think about your higher potential. Imagine what your higher potential might feel like. And see what kind of image crops up in your mind. What would you most like to be and what does that look like?"

And that was the moment we were born, a completely unrealistic butterfly hatching from a cocoon, showing off its wings in the sun and flying away. Yes, thought Muriel, to unfold my wings and fly away, that's what I want. I want to fly away. She felt a pleasant warmth deep in her belly and smiled as she made us crawl out of the cocoon a few times and fly away.

"Have you found your image?" Muriel asked.

"Yes," said Muriel.

"Lovely." Melodie breathed slowly and emphatically in and out a few more times. "Very good, Muriel. If you like, you can now tell me what you can see. But you can also keep it to yourself. Whatever you prefer."

"Hmm, hmm," said Muriel, totally absorbed in the wealth of colours in our wings, and the warm yellow of the rising sun we were flying towards.

"The advantage is that if you share it, we can use it in the therapy. It can give us both guidance. Like a kind of dot on the horizon."

And with those last words, we were driven towards a flashing red dot in Muriel's mind's eye, and she opened her eyes and described as well as she could what we looked like.

"Wow, Muriel! How remarkable! That's a very beautiful image to work towards together. That's really inspirational. And do you have any idea yourself what is currently getting in the way of you opening your beautifully coloured wings and flying away?"

Muriel was bursting with ideas as to what might be in the way, and Melodie was totally confident she could help her to clear away those obstacles, but in retrospect we can say that over the years that followed she didn't fly towards us but away; she lost rather than gained colour and beauty; lost warmth, lost strength. She was more like a moth flying into a hot lamp than a butterfly towards the rising sun.

Despite the fact we had tried our hardest. We were as clear as we could be. We tried to show her in the way we crawled out of the cocoon and flew, away, towards freedom. Watch, we said, watch, Muriel, this is what freedom looks like. But we couldn't show her how we got there because Muriel didn't think about what had preceded our emerging as a butterfly, about what we'd needed as a tiny imaginary caterpillar to become big enough to be able to calmly spin ourself into a cocoon, grow wings, and wait until they were ready to open.

You need food to be able to fly, Muriel! A slice of bread with chocolate sprinkles perhaps. But Muriel sees things differently.

That first day, Melodie had already said that whatever Muriel did she shouldn't take the image of her complete potential too literally, she was free to interpret its meaning any way she liked. And the metaphorical Hungry Caterpillar inside her was not looking for food for her body but food for her soul, food Melodie gave her in colourful pre-cooked portions.

"You're very sensitive, Muriel; that part of you is not very well developed. You probably had a cerebral upbringing, I'm guessing?"

It was true when Muriel thought about it, and full of enthusiasm she told her old friends from Business School that Melodie had said that she was actually very sensitive, and the old friends listened and nodded and said "hmm" and "yes" at the right moments and "I can imagine," after which they asked about her holiday plans, and when Muriel shared her disappointment at their reaction with Melodie, Melodie explained that sensitive people are often met with incomprehension because others have never experienced such sensitivity and so find it hard to imagine what it's like to have to feel so much all the time, and also because most people are inclined to continually anaesthetize themselves with an excess of stimuli, which you can hardly blame them for, and maybe Muriel should ask herself how nourishing contact with people like that was for her, and the next time Muriel saw her friends, she came to the conclusion that the contact wasn't nourishing at all. This doesn't give me wings, she thought, and that thought arose more frequently in her mind—when she went for a stroll with colleagues from the tax advice office during the lunch break, during a group walking holiday with friends her age, while she was watching TV at home on the couch. This doesn't nourish me, she'd think then, this is actually rather empty. And she took more and more of a dislike to these things.

"What gives you wings? That's what you need to ask yourself," Melodie had said. And each time, the answer took her closer to Melodie and further from the rest of the world, until Muriel swapped her own living room for Melodie's, where from that moment on she pursued her higher potential together with Melodie, Petrus, and Elisabeth.

And there, in this living room, a couple of years later, we had to watch from our powerless position when Muriel was introduced to the idea that even food—real, edible, tangible food—no longer counted as food. It started with a film that Melodie had found on the internet, which showed a man and a woman, a little younger than Muriel and very happy with themselves, with each other, and with their two small children, and their happiness, they said, was due to the fact they had stopped eating a couple of years previously. Since then they'd experienced a much stronger connection with the universal life force, so that they had increasingly begun to live on "abundance," while at the same time they were able to spend less money and reduced their environmental footprint.

"Isn't that fantastic?" Melodie said when the film was over. "This gives me a very good feeling. This could well be the next step for us to realize our ideals. Don't you think so? Imagine what kind of world we could live in. Imagine what it would be like if everybody could directly absorb energy from light and air. What a beautiful pure world we'd live in then."

Light and air, Muriel. Light and air! You went to school, didn't you? You did learn to do sums? You do know that there are natural laws that we all have to obey whether we want to or not? Even a non-existent butterfly like us understands that.

And the worst thing was, if there was anyone who understood, it was Muriel. If there was anyone who could do maths, it was Muriel. No wonder the idea of stopping eating frightened her. No wonder she thought: but that's not possible, is it? People burn energy, don't they? Two thousand calories a day if they have a sedentary lifestyle. That's on all the packaging isn't it? That's just how it is.

But the people in the film did live without eating. And they were happy. They had become freer and lighter since they stopped eating. Light enough to fly away, thought Muriel, and I clearly haven't got that far, because my mind is holding me back with the restrictive thought that I'm dependent on food.

That is your clear-thinking, mathematical mind, Muriel! That is your mind—it *knows* that you can't live without food!

And although Muriel tried with all her might to put her clear-thinking mind to rest about it, it didn't give in, fortunately, and persisted in raising objections to Melodie's plan. So Muriel used her laptop time to secretly google how many calories people needed to survive and how long people could last on a starvation diet, and when the group started eating less in preparation for the nine-day process, she began to add up how much energy the foodstuffs she ate comprised, and how many calories she burned when she sat, sang, walked, stood, or cleaned the house, and she thought of ways to limit the energy use to a minimum, for example by thinking as little as possible, because brains need a lot of sugar, she'd read, and she developed a strategy for thinking less and distracting herself from the hunger at the same time, by very slowly and as consciously as possible counting back from a hundred to zero.

Think as little as possible, Muriel? What do *you* think? Do you think we *don't* think? Do you think we don't have to run our small but delicate nervous system at full power to achieve the complex alignment between body and wings and air which is necessary to be able to take off from the leaf we are sitting on? Do you really think you will be able to unfold your wings without using your brain?

Light-winged as we may look, so heavy-hearted we

feel when we see Muriel doing one of her sums, only to hear her say to herself that she shouldn't depend on sums so much; when we hear her ask herself for the umpteenth time why she still has to be so obsessive about food.

Because you are hungry, Muriel! Because your body is asking for food. Because the only good thing for you is to do what you've been longing to do all morning. If you'd just stop counting down from a hundred to zero and put that sandwich in your mouth.

Clearly she has to be locked up in a prison cell first to understand that she needs food, because now she finally folds over the slice of bread and brings it to her mouth using both hands and takes a large bite from the middle, and another bite, and another one. The chocolate sprinkles that fall gather in her lap, in the groove between her thighs, where they immediately begin to melt, but that doesn't matter. First eat, Muriel. Food for your wings, fuel for your brain. And don't forget to chew before you swallow.

11

We are a cello, a lonely cello no longer played. Through the sides of the case, the walls of the room, the house in which we are confined, we listen to the sounds from outside, of birds, dogs, people, and engines—it is hard to differentiate the four through all these barriers. Still, we do our best to be able to hear them. They form our last point of contact with life.

It's been so long now since we've seen light, felt human hands, brought forth music, that we sometimes wonder whether we still exist. After years of neglect, it looks like Melodie has abandoned us for good. Like a worn-out pair of shoes. While we are anything but worn out. Our sound has become more powerful over the centuries. Deeper, more robust, richer in overtones. We were already like that when Melodie got us, and over the years she played us our sound became even richer, but despite this, there came a time when she put us aside, though she's never gone so far as to sell us or give us away. Still, one day she left us in this junk room and hasn't touched us since.

They always say it's not possible, love at first sight, that it's only later when love has blossomed that you rewrite the first encounter as a moment of immediate recognition, and of course we're fairly romantically minded but we swear that as soon as we heard the tinkle of the shop's bell we knew that there she was, our new player. She must have been eighteen, or maybe even only seventeen. Our previous owner, a middle-aged man with too much money and too little musicality, who thank god had finally realized we were too good for the hobbyism he exhibited towards us, had sold us back to the violin maker just a few days earlier, and we happened to be on his workbench for a full overhaul when Melodie, her father, and her cello teacher came into the shop.

What a stroke of luck, we often thought later, that the violin maker didn't put us down when he walked from his workshop into the shop to assist his customers. What a stroke of luck that he'd already cleaned and restrung us, and that we lay in his hands, shiny and ready to be played.

"That one. I'll take that one," Melodie said at once, then looked at the men on either side of her, shocked at herself, and then to the third man behind the counter. "Um," she said to the violin maker, "because we're looking for a new cello."

"A new cello. That's lucky, because if you were looking for a tuba I wouldn't recommend this one," the violin maker replied, and the three men burst out laughing, though we didn't really understand why, and Melodie didn't either by the looks of it and her cheeks turned red. The men became serious again at once. The violin maker wanted to know what kind of quality they were looking for, to which Melodie's father coughed meaningfully and said they were looking for a serious cello, something approaching concert quality, because his daughter would be attending the Royal Conservatoire from September, if she got in, but of course everyone assumed she would.

The violin maker nodded approvingly. "Then this could indeed be a suitable instrument for her," he said, and he laid us in Melodie's hands.

So young they were, those hands, so young. A fraction of our own age. But as soon as they took us, we felt in her essence something a little older than us, a vulnerability, a longing, the same thing that once drove humans to build cellos. These hesitant hands, whose fingertips tenderly slid along our strings, from our scroll to our bridge, who placed us with concentration between her knees, took up the bow, placed it against the A-string, and drew, these hands felt as if they knew what music is, what art is, what beauty is. The air was laden with potential, with the chemistry between us, the instrument entrusted to her, and this young woman; a chemistry that could take her cello-playing to great heights.

Perhaps this all sounds rather lofty to you, but don't forget we're offspring of the Baroque era, important offspring too, perhaps the most important creation from that period. One of the few inventions that have stood the test of time across the centuries, be it with minor technical adaptations and improvements, but basically intact, and whose antique examples often function better than those produced today. Of course, we're not the only musical instrument to be invented in that period; we don't want to deny or trivialise the existence of other instruments, but, without placing ourselves in the foreground, we still have to conclude that we are the best instrument. There's a reason that cellos are some of the most expensive instruments in the world. The cello most resembles a human being without being one. It doesn't have the arrogance of a violin, which places itself at the centre of the symphonic universe, seeming to forget that there are other musical instruments here on earth. A cello, on the other hand, is capable of performing solos and excelling as the composer of our longings, while still able to offer support and grounding to our less solid-sounding colleagues with just as much dedication.

And Melodie understood us. She played with a combination of restraint and surrender, that first time. You felt her wanting it, to lose herself in the music, and at the same time there was reserve, doubt, insecurity in terms of placing her fingertips and using the bow. A combination of fear of playing the wrong notes, concern for the dynamics, and being over-conscious of the listening ears of the three men: her father, the cello teacher, the instrument maker, each with their own musical preferences and their unquestioning assumption that their preferences were right for themselves and for others, and that they were the right person to judge the playing of anyone whatsoever.

Pointless concerns because Melodie was not being judged that afternoon—it was about us, the sounds we would be able to bring forth in her hands. Not to make things overly painful for her old cello, which she had brought to the shop to exchange and who lay silently in its case, preparing itself for the coming parting, we tried to respond discreetly to her touch, not to give everything at once or resonate too enthusiastically in the upper registers, but at the same time be warm and clear enough to demonstrate how good we were. Not to make the old cello, which was certainly adequate for its price range, jealous, but to win Melodie's heart and the approval of the men who were deciding whether or not to purchase us.

Melodie was immediately sold; the men needed a little longer. They forced her to try out two cheaper examples first because we were a little above the budget, but the cello teacher judged, finally, that we had the most potential.

"We can make the step to Conservatory level with this one," he said. And to her father, "You might not be able to hear the difference right away when she plays but it really is a better instrument. If this inspires her to play better, and more than that to listen to herself better, it would be a shame to walk away from that for a thousand guilders more than a lesser cello. And this could be an instrument for life for her, if she ever starts working as a professional."

Melodie's father nodded slowly as he paid close attention to her. We felt her fingers become sweaty; her left hand gripped our neck a little more tightly. "An arm and a leg," he said. "Alright, go on then. But I'll be expecting you to pay me back for this investment with dedication to your musical studies, young lady."

And with this our future together was sealed. A rollercoaster future, we could say. For better or for worse we stuck with her, but when we look back now we mainly remember the worse.

Melodie, who ruined her audition at the Royal Conservatoire in The Hague due to her nerves and had to make do with a place at the one in Utrecht. Melodie, who told her classmates that she played for the music and not for success, but who practised until she was blue in the face in the meantime, all for a pat on the back from her cello teacher. Melodie, who failed her first-year exams, ran home in panic, and with her father's help lodged a complaint against the music school board's assessment, after which she was given a second chance and allowed to go through to the second year, during which she studied even more frantically. Melodie, looked upon pityingly by her housemates because she'd burst out crying if anyone criticised her or cracked a mean joke. Melodie, who wanted to believe in something higher, something more beautiful, better—and that in the godless 1980s when the universe most young people lived in was completely vacuous. Melodie, who thought it shouldn't be about being the best, but who, nevertheless, always wanted to be better than all the rest.

Melodie, during her finals. She didn't play badly, if you knew that her hands had been shaking so much an hour before that she was barely capable of pressing her Valium pills from their packet. She overdramatised when she played, she always had done, we had to agree with her cello teacher about that. She was overly fond of her vibrato. But the love she poured into her playing was genuine and that's why she always won back our sympathy, as well as that of the very human people in the assessment committee, those who argued for passing her, while the stricter ones would have had her retake the exam. And they had a point, she wasn't a great cellist when it came to nuances, particularly during performances and exams when the fear of making mistakes affected her fine-motor skills so much that the dynamic changes always came across as a little too crude, or too abrupt. And of course that isn't the best basis for playing the cello professionally, in any case not at the highest level, but when we finally learned that she'd scored a basic pass, we still hoped there would be a fine future ahead of us with her, as the cello of a passionate cello teacher.

It wasn't an easy time, her college years, not for her and not for us. But in retrospect it didn't go properly downhill until after that, when Melodie no longer had any teachers and had to manage on her own with just us. She did start giving cello lessons in order to earn money, as we'd expected. But why she chose to teach children, we still don't understand. Because children are so uninhibited, we once heard her say to someone, but she couldn't cope at all with the capriciousness of the uninhibited infant brain. They didn't listen to her, and if they listened they didn't understand her, and they didn't practice, they didn't progress, and when the mothers and fathers came to pick up their little mites, they blamed Melodie for their children not learning anything. We were only used for playing separate notes and children's tunes. She lost heart. She no longer overdramatised. She no longer made a single sound on us that could be felt, or that conveyed anything other than disinterest combined with existential despair. And a broken heart, because during that period, her girlfriend, the woman she'd lived with since graduating, had only gone and left her as well.

When, one day, Melodie decided not to go to the music school, we had hoped that better times were ahead. That she'd get the time and space to play us for pleasure again. That she'd rediscover her love of vibrato. But instead she stopped playing entirely. She scarcely did anything. She ate and slept. We were with her all day but she didn't want to touch us. She lay on the sofa under a blanket, and we stood in our case, propped up next to the bookshelf. If only she'd taken us out of our case, just once. If only she'd tried, tried to play us just once like that very first time. We could have given her all the consolation she needed. But she distanced herself from us. We did hear her talking on the phone, about some kind of therapy she was following to connect more with her feelings. "I feel such an aversion when I think of that cello," she said. "Such aversion. All the years I tied myself in knots trying to make that thing sound like it was supposed to. I've ended up so distanced from my own feelings." When we heard that, one of our strings spontaneously snapped. We never forced her to tie herself in knots, and still she blamed us. Then she convinced herself that she was more interested in human contact than in music. That coaching others through the process of change she had undergone was more her thing than performing the work of dead composers. That she'd rather see music as a means than a goal. And then she moved us from the sitting room to the junk room.

It was quiet for years after that. How she managed, we don't know, she was home a lot, she lived like a ghost. Until those other people moved into the house one day. Soon after which she bought a whole range of Renaissance musical instruments.

What a shame, a crying shame. This can only end badly, that much is clear. There isn't a single sound in the house now. Melodie has gone, her house-mates too. The police who searched the house have left. Everyone has gone and we've been forgotten. But we are not yet lost. As long as we can still hear the outside world, we don't lose hope. Be patient. Wait for this phase to end, for someone to lift us out of our case, replace our broken string, our rosin, and tighten our bow, place our sound box between their knees and allow us to sing again.

12

We are two cigarettes. We don't know each other, we weren't made in the same factory, but we are still connected, the way all cigarettes are connected to each other, so we can always feel when there's another cigarette in the vicinity, and right now the pair of us are only a few dozen metres apart, and quite coincidentally we are lit at the exact same moment. Petrus, in the small, still, cool courtyard of the cell complex where he is getting some air, inhales the smoke through the filter into his lungs as though taking his first ever breath. The combustion products in our carefully assembled mixture of ingredients fill his lungs and, in this burning form, we diffuse from his alveoli into his blood, circulate throughout his body, and penetrate his brain where all kinds of things are going on.

Since smoking his first cigarette in years yesterday, after the questioning, he can no longer think about anything else. Only about us, and Liesbeth, who is smoking her own cigarette, two floors up in the full sun on the police station roof—Petrus doesn't know she's called Liesbeth, only that the scent of smoke lingered around her, and that she'd given him disbelieving looks after every answer he gave during the questioning.

"Your housemate lies dying before your eyes and you think of nothing."

This sentence continues to echo inside his head, banging against the walls of his skull and multiplying in every direction. And you think nothinggg ... somethinggg ... nooothinggg ...

No, he thinks. No. I thought nothing. And I did nothing. This time I really didn't do anything at all. I didn't hit or shove anyone. I didn't even scream. And that must be a good thing, that I controlled myself, that I stayed calm, present in the moment. But even if I do nothing, it's not good. Everyone is against me.

Particularly that Liesbeth. She was very, very against him, in a very frustrating manner. Not angry, but amazed, even astonished maybe. As though she couldn't follow things using her logic. And the worst thing is he has to agree with her. It actually sounds very logical that you shouldn't think nothing when your housemate lies there dying. You shouldn't be quiet then, but should scream. And he wonders whether he actually shouldn't have screamed a lot sooner and more often. Shouldn't he have screamed at Melodie that this wasn't a solution—not smoking, not drinking, not eating, not screaming. Abstaining from everything that offered release, except for singing, that sad sweet singing, which did allow for energy to escape, but in a manner more like air from a leaking tyre slowly hissing out. That's the way he feels now, like a flat tyre deflating. And he puts our filter between his lips to fill himself again. A new dose of nicotine finds its way to his brain. His blood vessels constrict. Adrenaline, dopamine, and serotonin are released. This is relaxation. Pure relaxation for only thirty cents per cigarette. Like Petrus we are wondering how he could have lived without us for so long. How he could ever have thought, as he did only yesterday, that we weren't good for him.

"Trust your feelings," he hears Melodie say, and Petrus feels that what he is doing is good. The inner peace we bring to him is unrivalled. He only needs two drags to come to himself again, after a period of years in which it was clear he had totally lost the plot. How many people would lose their minds if they didn't have us; we don't have any hard figures but Petrus offers undeniable anecdotal evidence. If he'd just kept on smoking he never would have gone along with the plan to stop eating.

And we haven't talked about Liesbeth yet, taking her third drag on the police-station roof, sharing unconsciously with Petrus the knowledge that we will save them, not from death, not from illness—they both know that people claim we cause fatal illnesses, though there are other things that aren't healthy long-term either—but from their discomfort, their anger and their fear. They are prepared to put up with the residue we leave behind in their lungs for what we have to offer: a pleasant moment of finally being able to think clearly. While the echo of "and you think nothing" sounds in Petrus's thoughts, Liesbeth turns over the image of Petrus during the questioning. The way he sat on the edge of his seat, shoulders pulled up, hands balled into fists, eyes turned down, mute and voiceless. Like a moody child, she thinks, because without her realizing, since her daughter got sick she's seen a child in everyone. And as with her own child she feels a combination of incomprehension and rage; she wanted to take him by the shoulders and shout, "What's the problem? What is it? Speak! Explain it to me."

Yesterday evening, after the examination, when she was sitting at the garden table with her daughter, the image had inverted itself. Observing her daughter, who sat in front of her plate of food with the same raised shoulders and balled fists, she'd suddenly seen Petrus. She had suddenly realized that her world was as far removed from her daughter's as it was from Petrus Zwarts's; that the reasons Nina had withdrawn into herself went beyond her powers of comprehension, and that there wasn't much use in expecting more from her daughter than from this impenetrable suspect in an even more impenetrable case.

"That's the difficult thing about vulnerable suspects," Asif had said after the session. "We don't know their backstory. So we don't actually have the faintest idea what kinds of things have caused their fears and confusion. We can only see that they are frightened and confused and try to respond to that as best we can. And nobody frightened and confused was ever calmed down by anger or coercion."

And although she had felt slight annoyance at the tone he used, the comment had come to mind that evening again as she watched her daughter, and it had made her more tolerant. Unlike previous evenings, she hadn't got into a heated discussion about how many mouthfuls her daughter should eat. She'd only asked her daughter once if she was really sure she didn't want anything else, and after that she'd calmly finished the food on her own plate, cleared the table, put the food that should have been in her daughter's stomach in the organic waste container—knowing that otherwise it would simply take a detour into the toilet—and had gone to smoke a cigarette. And with the same leniency as yesterday evening, she wrote up her report on Petrus this morning, and now she's on the roof, enjoying her moment with us, ignoring the burning heat of the sun, and thinking about vulnerable people. Her daughter is vulnerable but in a very different way from Petrus. The strength she sees in her daughter, the dedication with which Nina is starving herself, seems totally absent in Petrus. While her daughter uses all she has got to resist the commanding looks around her, to be able to decide herself how little she eats, even when she's told it will kill her, Petrus seems to have given up all resistance. He didn't stop eating to take back self-control, no, he passed on that authority to others, and that's why he didn't eat, because the group had chosen not to. Not to rebel against those around him, but out of a lack of resistance. And if Liesbeth brings together everything she has read and heard up to this point, the same is true of Elisabeth—Elisabeth was even more susceptible to the influence of her surroundings than this Petrus. So it wasn't her choice to stop eating but the choice of those around her. And that, decides Liesbeth, really shouldn't be allowed, that someone who is so impressionable should be urged to do something that would kill them, encouraged by those around her. Leading people who are vulnerable to suggestion unresistingly along the path to death by starvation, now that should be forbidden. The law ought to, no, the law *must* intervene, Liesbeth tells herself as she grips our filter a little tighter. She resolves to do everything she can to gather the necessary evidence that the victim didn't act out of free will, and that the people around her have done something punishable by law, namely letting a person with no will of her own die of hunger. A person who needed help and instead was prescribed a deadly diet. And in Liesbeth's mind, the people who prescribed it deserved to pay.

And if it's up to Petrus, someone will have to pay for what happened, even though he is thinking more of the fact that he has been arrested than of Elisabeth's death. Someone or something will have to pay. Perhaps simply this wall he is leaning against; maybe he can give it a few big kicks. But he doesn't. He has just enough self-control to take another drag instead and to stand still. He thinks of the woman again, of Liesbeth, who gave him such disbelieving looks as she ascertained that he had thought of nothing while his housemate lay dying. He'd like to kick her, or at least shake her hard, to make it clear that it wasn't his fault, that he's not the guilty one. For her to realize that he really tried his hardest all those years. He thought that this was the best thing to do. He'd wanted to stop hitting and kicking and screaming. And perhaps he has still screamed a lot in recent years, but he hasn't kicked or hit, not any people anyway. And that must be worth something. Someone should really praise him for that some time, that he hasn't got into any fights, or woken up drunk on a roadside, and that he hasn't been fired from any jobs since he moved in with Melodie. Because he hasn't had a job, that's true, but anyway. They never sent him away. He never acted so badly that they wanted him gone. And perhaps he did have to give up too much for this and went along with Melodie too much. But he worked so hard. He had to do so much to keep himself in check. It would have been asking too much to expect him to look out for Elisabeth as well. They all had their challenges they had to contend with. It was Melodie's job, making sure that everything went well with everyone. She was the therapist. Maybe not officially, officially they were equal housemates, but in practice she was. She was the one with the most understanding.

Or not, he suddenly thinks, as he inhales his last drag and extinguishes his cigarette butt on the wall. Maybe she wasn't the one with the most understanding. But how was I supposed to know that? And with that question he blows the smoke into the warm summer air, where it will mix with the last smoke Liesbeth is exhaling on the roof, and as our stubs are left behind each in a different ashtray, our smokers, their bodies and souls anointed, go back indoors.

13

We are Elisabeth's body. We are cold. We never got this cold when Elisabeth was still alive, though we often had difficulty keeping our extremities warm in recent years, but even so, the temperature of our heart and other vital organs never went below thirty-seven degrees. We made sure of that.

But now that life has slipped out of us, despite all our exertions, we are at the mercy of other forces, the forces from the warm, still-living bodies, who lifted us from her airbed onto a bus on a stretcher and drove us to this place, this strange building filled with rooms with stainless-steel surfaces, with more bodies like us, stored in life-sized cooled drawers. They want to stop us decomposing, preserve us exactly the way we were just before Elisabeth stopped breathing. Keep liquids in their reservoirs, remove from hungry bacteria the desire to reproduce, have dying cells pause in their process of wizening, everything to keep intact the traces of the series of events that led to Elisabeth's death. We do pretty much understand, but it's not nice, this cold.

That aside, it is very pleasing to be in the hands of the Forensic Institute's most passionate pathologist, Theo van den Lijstbeek, who is now staring at us, together with his technical assistant. "Bodies don't lie, son," he says. "The dead have gone for ever but the bodies remain behind with all the information."

Bodies don't lie, that's true, but Elisabeth didn't lie much when she was alive either, because she hardly spoke, so anyone giving us a full investigation will probably end up knowing more than all the people who tried to talk to her those last years of her life. In any case we haven't heard her say anything in a long time that wasn't just repeating another's words. The truth about what was going on inside her stayed inside her, inside us.

But now there's Theo, and Theo is better than anyone at slicing information out of us with his scalpel, though he'll probably concentrate on the cause of her death, which is a shame, we feel, them being so fixated on that, out of Elisabeth's long life wanting to know more than anything how it ended rather than how it was lived. The way a person dies does say something about their life, though, and in Elisabeth's case, it definitely does.

Whatever Theo is required to investigate, we are in the best possible hands with him, we don't doubt that. We sensed it immediately when he and his assistant took us out of the cold store. The care with which he slid his hand under our shoulders, the cautiousness with which he supported our spine as they moved us onto the dissection table. Being touched in this way is not something we were able to experience during Elisabeth's lifetime. We were largely deprived of contact with other bodies. It never got beyond the platonic with that one boyfriend she had, aside from the odd stroke under the bedcovers; and the odd person held her hand in recent years but that mainly felt a bit awkward.

And now we are lying here entirely exposed, in total surrender, let's say, on our backs with our dead skin on the cold stainless steel, while the forensic photographer takes pictures of us.

"Look at those bones," Theo says with a twinkle in his eye. "Beautiful in fact, such a clear skeletal structure. You don't see that often."

The photographer nods absentmindedly, absorbed in his work. He's also passionate about his job, but not about us. Not like Theo is.

"The beauty of the human body continues to amaze me," says Theo as he studies us from every angle, from close up and from a distance. He glances at his assistant, "Pay close attention today, Floris. We're going to do everything completely according to the book."

If only during her life Elisabeth had had half as much reverence for us, her own body, as Theo now, then we wouldn't be lying here. If she'd displayed a quarter of his care, an eighth of his passion, a six-teenth of his willingness to make us comfortable, she would still have been alive. We gave off all pos-sible signals to make it clear what we needed. At the end we'd pulled our stomach into a continuous spasm in the hope that the shooting pain would make her change her mind. We made stars and black patches appear in her field of vision. We let our legs wobble, our knees buckle, our lungs constrict. We stopped producing saliva. But none of it helped. She didn't respond. Of course, this was also because she was no longer in a fit state to think at the end, as we were so busy staying alive that we didn't have enough glucose left to allow our brain to function normally.

The photographer has finished. Theo and the technical assistant take over. The assistant is given the honour of measuring and weighing us as Theo types the numbers into his computer, shaking his head as he does. Then he returns to the dissection table. We feel the warmth of his approaching body. He doesn't undress us with his eyes, we are naked already after all, but instead he strips the skin from our flesh with his eyes so that he can picture what is underneath it.

"Right, first a quick look from close up." He bends over us and his gentle gloved fingers palpitate our neck, our shoulders, arms, hands. He traces our past life. Bruising, scratches, wounds, minuscule holes in the skin made by needles. He opens our mouth and asks his assistant to shine a light into it. Lifts up our eyelids, looks up our nose. Into our ears. He feels our scalp underneath our hair with his fingertips. Then he quickly checks the rest of our body: chest and belly, legs and feet.

"Shall we turn her onto her side?"

Now we are lying on our left side, kept in balance by the technical assistant as we feel Theo's warm breath pass along our spine and down the backs of our legs.

"No, no contusions or abrasions here either. No visible traces of violence, medicine, or drugs use— would you note that down? And then she can be laid onto her back again." A hand on our hip as he guides our back onto the cold dissection surface again.

"Good, very good. Then we'll take a look at the inside of this lady."

The way he looks at us is unforgettable. We've never been regarded with so much eagerness. If we could still move, we'd be shaking with happiness, but unfortunately all we can do is continue to lie motionless and surrender to a little dream about what it would have been like if Elisabeth had met someone like Theo when she was alive. Someone who looked at us, saw us. Someone who touched us like that. How delicious that would have been, if we forget for a moment that Theo would never have been this interested in us if Elisabeth had still been alive, because then he wouldn't have been able to do with her what he likes to do best, without hurting her, and we don't have him down as the kind of man who likes to hurt women, he's too gentle for that, you can tell from the way he cuts, slowly and unobtrusively; two cuts to the side from our breastbone and one straight down from the middle of our belly to the start of our vagina. He cuts with respect, not aiming to break us but on the contrary to keep us as attractive as possible for when he sews us up again later.

For the first time in our existence light falls on our insides, bright white scientific light. For the first time we are touched on the inside. The assistant holds our skin aside as Theo saws through our breastbone with slow concentration to reach the organs within our rib cage. He takes our heart in one hand as he cuts through the veins and arteries that connect it to the rest with the other. He takes it out of our chest and passes it to the assistant who rinses away the remaining blood under the tap, before weighing it and placing it on the dissection table. Theo picks up our heart, holds it in his gloved hands, and brings it up to his face. "I understand why you stopped beating," he says. "How much did it weigh?"

"One hundred and ninety-eight grams."

Theo slowly nods. "The weight of a dog's heart." Is that sadness we can hear beneath the tone of factual observation in his voice? Indignation? "That's quite something. I've had enough manhandled bodies on the table but I still find it incomprehensible that people treat their own bodies like this."

"Are you thinking suicide?"

Theo lays our heart on the dissection table so that the photographer can take a picture of it. "We're going to look into everything as carefully as possible and rule out what we can. But it would surprise me if we turned up anything other than malnutrition. And given I don't see any signs of force or coercion, it looks like this lady did it to herself."

Or as we would say: she did this to *us*. Though we wouldn't be able to maintain absolutely that there wasn't any coercion. We're only a simple body and we don't know everything about the world of Elisabeth's mind but we can remember that Elisabeth couldn't say or do anything in recent years without being criticised or corrected, and we think this is one of the reasons that she slowly but surely began to listen to us less and less. When Theo looks in our throat, he'll probably discover that there isn't much left of the muscles around our vocal chords. And say he deviated from standard procedure and subjected our hands to further investigation, if he cut open the skin of our fingers and hands and studied the muscle tissue, he'd discover that the muscles were unusually well-developed there, much stronger than you'd expect from a person who didn't seem to know what it was to fight for something, but that was because this made her better able to fight against something, namely us, against all the longings inside us, and she did that with balled fists, hidden inside the pockets of her massively oversized coat or sweater or cardigan, each time we told her she was hungry or thirsty or needed to stretch her legs or wanted to cuddle up to a stranger in the train. There, in the muscles of our hands, all her unfulfilled longings are stored. And why exactly Elisabeth decided one day to listen to someone else rather than us, we don't entirely understand, but we do know that there are cleverer, more subtle ways of getting someone to do something than by physical force, more effective ways to compel a person to fight against their bodily impulses.

But those more subtle ways don't count for Theo. He's only interested in what happened inside of us. He studies each of our organs, one by one. He cuts them free, gives them to his assistant to weigh, searches for abnormalities. Liver, stomach, intestines, kidneys. All much smaller than they should be. Atrophied, atrophied, atrophied. No further signs of illness. Of course not, because actually we were very healthy. We had the potential to live for a very long time. But Elisabeth sacrificed us, bit by bit, assisted by the people around her, those she had decided to listen to.

"I'll help you," we can still hear her sister saying. "I'll help you, but then you will have to *let* me help."

And then Elisabeth would ball her fists, but that didn't help and that's why we are lying here with Theo, who by now has looked inside our chest and stomach cavities and cut away a small section of each organ so he can study it under the microscope later. We like this idea, that a few significant pieces of us will stay behind here, close to this man, who genuinely seems well-disposed toward us, quite unlike the person who once lived inside. We can't read Theo's mind but we suspect that's the reason he doesn't hand off to his assistant and decides to close us himself. Not for the next of kin but for us, because we are still there, the silent witness of the way in which a person, whether coerced or not, is able to deny their body until the only thing it can do is surrender to death. And however sad we find that, there is still a certain happiness in us because if Elisabeth had stayed alive we never would have known what it was like to be touched inside by a loving hand.

14

We are the Hellingens.

Anja: Heard the news??? >:'-(
Maarten: Yeah shit
Johan: just back from dads. very sad
Maarten: Unbelievable. WTF!?
Johan: that it could come to this
Anja: BItch
Anja: Ssorry
Johan: yeah must be hard for her now too
Maarten: Rightly so. Jesus. Your own sister!
Anja: Wonder whether I should have said
   something at dads bday
Maarten: Wouldn't have helped. You know
   Melodie …
Anja: Sat down and wrote a really long email that
   night
Anja: That that living on light woman is a
   charlatan
Anja: Its all over the internet
Johan: I did call them the next day
Anja: I thought if I send all the links
Johan: about all that stuff she said to dad
Anja: About dementia you mean?

Maarten: Couldn't believe dad invited them in the first place. Wasn't the first time, was it?

Johan: yeah

Anja: Yeah that was heavy

Anja: But I never sent the email

Anja: Ed said it wasn't wise

Johan: prob right

Maarten: All the crazy stuff dad told me they'd said to him.

Anja: But what did she say to you Johan?

Maarten: I would've just disinherited her.

Johan: hmmm hard to recall

Johan: more or less the same old story

Johan: that they were trying to live together more intensely and we'd never learned that as kids

Johan: and that we're not in touch with nature either

Johan: and thats why dad forces mum to take medicine

Maarten: How does she get this stuff into her head?

Johan: she wanted to speak her own truth more

Johan: and she felt I was trying to stop her by calling her after

Johan: and I had no right to speak because I'm a man

Johan: because she felt dad was less strict with me and Maarten

Anja: Well ...

Maarten: What?

Anja: Well it wasn't really equal of course

Anja: You never had to help around the house

Maarten: Ouch. OK but it was like that back then.

Anja: Sure and it's all so long ago. There are worse things

Maarten: I don't think she ever had to help either.

Maarten: She always had to practice didn't she?

Anja: Oh yeah

Maarten: If anyone was given preferential treatment by dad it was her. Christ.

Johan: hey, do you mind?

Maarten: Oh pardon me, Reverend ;)

Anja: But did you talk to her about eating as well Johan?

Anja: After dads bday

Johan: well I did say that I thought it was rude to dad not to eat anything at all

Maarten: Plain bad manners right?

Maarten: First insisting that those other two nutters came along, dad having to cough up double, and then all four of them send their plates back to the kitchen.

Anja: But nothing about their health

Maarten: The cheek of it really.

Johan: health?

Anja: You didn't say it was dangerous, not eating?

Johan: no not specifically

Maarten: Jesus Christ you don't really think you have to explain to someone that it's dangerous not to eat …

Johan: Maarten.

Maarten: Sorry Johan but I'm angry. My sister died yeah?

Johan: but can you do that without taking the lord's name in vain

Johan: I take that as an insult

Maarten: I'll just shut up then

Anja: Because I was really terribly shocked when I saw what they looked like

Anja: I sat next to Elisabeth and her thighs were about as thin as my arms ...

Johan: and she was really turned inward. I prayed for her a lot afterwards. and for Melodie too

Anja: But shouldn't we have got her out of there?

Johan: because she is suffering too, we mustnt forget that

Johan: Elisabeth? from Melodie's?

Maarten: I can't believe we're having this conversation

Anja: I talked to Ed about that afterwards

Maarten: How is this possible?

Johan: you mean because of not eating?

Maarten: Why would you have to protect one sister from the other? What kind of nonsense is this?

Anja: Ed works with people like them you know

Maarten: With nutcases?

Anja: Anorexics

Johan: he thought it was anorexia?

Anja: He saw similarities

Johan: I thought that was only teenagers

Anja: We talked about that too

Maarten: Or Melodie never got past puberty?

Anja: About what Melodie was like as a teenager

Maarten: You don't need to be a shrink to see that Anja

Maarten: An ambitious cellist blind to the rest of the world.

Anja: Remember how she was just before her audition?

Maarten: Weepy, fucked up, unbearable ...

Anja: Come on Maarten she's still our sister

Johan: I think I'd already left home

Anja: Yeah Elisabeth had already left too. But she was very skinny back then already

Anja: At dads birthday I suddenly remembered cycling to school with her one time

Johan: Melodie you mean?

Anja: That massive cello on her back

Anja: She had to get off on that stretch along the canal because she couldn't handle the headwind

Anja: Who else

Johan: because you were talking about Elisabeth's legs just now

Anja: Yes but that's the worst thing because Elisabeth wasn't ambitious like Melodie at all

Anja: She was a bit quiet maybe but I never got the idea that there was anything wrong with her

Johan: but dad didn't breathe down her neck all the time

Maarten: Breathe down her neck? Worship you mean? Melodie was his be all and end all. And the fortune he spent on that cello.

Johan: I don't know Maarten. yes if she played well she was praised but if he didn't think it was good enough she was criticized just as harshly

Maarten: Oh like that is it? Poor damaged Melodie.

Johan: Maarten

Maarten: Dad always supported and encouraged her. He even went to the music academy that time when she failed the year.

Maarten: What? I didn't even say Jesus.

Maarten: And he must have criticized her then ...

Maarten: He criticized all of us anyway. He gave us what for if we came home with bad grades. No it wasn't all fun and games but he did mean well. And look where it got us. The three of us have landed on our feet.

Anja: Hey but I only wanted to say that Ed did think there were anorexic tendencies, the way Melodie acted back then

Johan: and Elisabeth?

Anja: Elisabeth used to be normal as a kid I think

Anja: Before she had a breakdown

Maarten: She never had much of a sense of humour

Anja: But some of dads jokes were harsh

Anja: The ones about mum

Johan: he wasn't always the most tactful no

Anja: I never found them funny

Maarten: But she *was* a terrible cook

Johan: he didn't need to remind everyone about it every day

Maarten: Everything was either raw or overcooked or burned

Anja: I think it was impotence on dads part

Maarten: And the way she went on about the environment all the time. No wonder he joked about it sometimes.

Anja: But Ed thought Melodie might have had a latent eating disorder back then

Anja: And if it doesn't escalate and is left untreated it can become a chronic kind of thing

Johan: ok but the housemates then? Anorexia isn't infectious

Anja: Yes but you can have collective psychosis

Anja: Ed thought it might be something like that. He checked to see if there was research on it but couldn't find anything

Anja: But Melodie is pretty dominant anyway

Maarten: You can say that again. And Elisabeth and those other two are completely spineless. That's why she picked them.

Anja: So yes we did talk about getting professional help

Anja: A social worker maybe. But we live quite a long way from them of course

Johan: hardly next door no

Anja: And Eds got enough on his plate at work

Johan: am I my brother's keeper?

Maarten: You know what gets my goat? It's too crazy for words ...

Johan: I lay awake asking myself that last night

Maarten: That you and Ed discussed this so much, and Ed even looked into the research, and you Johan were praying all the time, and all because Melodie was so determined to help Elisabeth.

Maarten: To help her! She kept going on about that. She was helping Elisabeth. But if she hadn't felt the need to help Elisabeth no help would have been necessary.

Maarten: Then Melodie could have stewed in her own juice with her eating disorder or her spiritual delusions or whatever it was and Elisabeth would still be alive.

Maarten: I mean it was hardly efficient

Maarten: Not to mention mum and dad, all they've had to suffer.

Johan: yes its very sad

Anja: Are there any plans for the funeral?

Johan: all those good intentions

Anja: Is dad going to arrange it or us?

Anja: Because I'm assuming Melodie can't do anything right now

Johan: depends. I called a few friends and they reckon the body will be released in a couple of days

Johan: and they don't think Melodie will be held for more than a couple of days either

Johan: I guess she'll want to arrange it herself then. But Bert said theres a way to prevent that if dad would rather do it

Maarten: Because actually as her father dad is the next of kin.

Anja: If I was dad I wouldnt bother getting into that fight

Johan: it could be quite tricky Bert said. because in principle the first person who contacts the undertakers automatically gets the right to arrange the funeral. but Melodie will probably be the first to know when the body is released.

Johan: and of course it would be more logical for Melodie to do it because she lived with Elisabeth for so long

Maarten: So what?

Maarten: If a man murders his wife he doesn't have the right to bury her because he lived with her does he?

Johan: that's not a nice comparison

Maarten: It's not that different

Johan: I don't like you comparing Melodie to a murderer

Johan: the police are still investigating it

Maarten: OK but in any case even if Melodie did spend the last decade with her those weren't the best years of her life.

Johan: and Melodie is our sister too

Maarten: So just because Melodie was the last person to see her doesn't mean she's the best person to lay her to rest.

Maarten: And Elisabeth has been our sister for more than fifty years too

Maarten: And mum and dad's daughter

Maarten: But if Melodie arranges it they won't pay any attention to that.

Johan: yes maybe thats the way it will go

Johan: but I want to leave it up to dad, whether he wants to prevent that or not

Anja: Would also cause a lot of fuss

Anja: And dads got enough on his mind

Maarten: Wonder whether she'll invite us.

Johan: she ought to

Maarten: Wouldn't be so sure.

Johan: if it turns out differently we could still get together for a memorial of our own

Anja: OK guys I have to go now but I was thinking one of us should stay in contact with dad about this right?

Maarten: I can do that

Anja: Johan?

Johan: sure I was going to anyway

Anja: Oh sorry Maarten didn't see your message, so who will?

Johan: I'm in touch with dad a lot because I'm
    dealing with the admin for mum going to the
    nursing home so I can just combine it
Maarten: Fine.
Anja: Great Johan. You'll keep us updated? I'm in
    the middle of a big job myself so working a lot of
    overtime in the evenings
Johan: will do
Anja: Super, thanks and speak soon
Maarten: Take care and good luck with work
Johan: be in touch
Anja: Thx 2 you too

15

We are the world wide web. We have answers to every question, even though, unfortunately, we cannot guarantee they are the right answers. But this doesn't stop most people from submitting to us their most pressing questions and deepest fears. Take Liesbeth: early this morning she sat down at her work computer and opened her browser, and not to ask us about work-related matters. The first thing we saw her type into the search bar was *how to handle daughter with anorexia*; after that she looked up *eating disorder support* and *forcing therapy eating disorders* and now she is busy going through the hits for *tips parents anorexia*. We've seen her visit these pages so often before but she clicks on them again so she can reread that patients with an eating disorder can only be helped if they want help themselves, the first step in this being that they are able to admit the existence of an eating disorder. She rereads how important it is not to get into an argument at every mealtime because it makes food even more of a sensitive topic for the patient. But at the same time one mustn't agree with the patient or go along with their delusion. She has the writers of the articles impress upon her once again that it's not her fault, that her first task is to take care of herself because the last thing the patient needs is for their nearest and dearest to be dragged down by it too. In addition, it is important not to blame the patient, because one needs to realize that an eating disorder is an illness and that this sickness is the reason the patient is behaving in such a deceitful and self-destructive way. The best thing relatives can do is remain accepting of the condition and provide regular opportunities to discuss the possibility of seeking help, once the patient has finally reached that point. And again, using the search terms *accept and avoid arguments delusory anorexia* and *discuss help anorexia* and *anger anorexia*, Liesbeth searches in vain for an answer to how you can remain accepting, how you can avoid arguments and not come across as accusatory without going along with someone's delusion, but this only takes her back to the stories she has already read. She scrolls and clicks around a bit, copies the phone numbers of two treatment centres and a support group into an email to herself labelled *call tonight!!!*, and presses send. Then she closes all the tabs and types: *Elisabeth van Hellingen.*

The name takes her straight to the website of the Sound & Love Commune where she hovers over a piece about Elisabeth's problems, written by Melodie, which explains that Elisabeth has always struggled to open up to other people due to unspecified events in the past. There are photos of Elisabeth with Melodie, Muriel, and Petrus, of Elisabeth alone with Melodie, of Melodie's compositions, coloured-in musical notes on hand-drawn staves, with the caption *composition Melodie van Hellingen, coloured in by Elisabeth.*

Liesbeth holds her cursor over the pictures for a while, tracing imaginary circles around Elisabeth's head. Then she clicks on a link at the top of the page, *Melodie's account*. She is redirected to Melodie's Facebook page and begins to look through Melodie's timeline, searching for the name Elisabeth, reading back in time; a couple of months, a year, two years until she reaches an account of the nine-day process. She reads the posts one by one, beginning with the first day and scrolling upwards after that.

Melodie van Hellingen

12th September 2016
Day 1 of the nine-day process

Today we started the nine-day process! In nine (three times three) days we are going to liberate ourselves from our dependence upon food. Over the coming period we'll be receiving online guidance twice a day from Maruko who lives in the United States. At the beginning the internet connection wasn't that stable but in general communication went smoothly. Aside from the four of us—me, Muriel, Petrus, and my sister Elisabeth, who also lives with us, there were two American men from Arizona and also a French woman who lives in Canada. So a very international group! Given the time difference it was handy for Maruko to do the first session when it was their morning and 3 a.m. for us, and the second session will be noon our time. We didn't mind getting up early for it and Maruko said we'd probably get more energy soon so that we wouldn't need as much sleep anyway. During the first session we started with a lovely ritual, laying down our intentions to reach a higher plane of consciousness. The affirmation (a kind of mantra that provides inspiration!) we were given for this was: "I will be nourished by the universe." What a beautiful starting point and it goes really well with what I've been feeling and experiencing myself for a long time. We also did about an hour and a half's breathing and light meditation led by Maruko. You can tell he has a lot of experience, the meditation went really deep. We immediately felt a strong connection even though there's an ocean between us. That's because of the similar wavelengths, Maruko said, and he noticed that as a group we picked up the same frequency really fast! Very nice to hear. I've put so much energy into this over the past years to get the group to a basic level and now we are reaping the rewards of this. Only drank juice the rest of the day and already feel very light, as if more energy is being freed.

Melodie van Hellingen

13th September 2016
Day 2

Today we were given more information on how the nine-day process is structured. Originally Maruko did the process in 30 days but after his own experiences he changed it to 9 days. The three days in the middle are entirely without food and drink and so the process is set up with perfect symmetry, which goes with the regular patterns you see in nature and the whole universe! Because what we are doing on a small scale also happens on a larger scale in the cosmos and is reflected again in our cells and even at an atomic level. This explanation was totally new for us but in keeping with what I have been intuiting for much longer! What a privilege to come into contact and share and expand wisdom with likeminded people in this way. Together with these people on the other side of the world we have set off on a very special journey and it seems as though we have left the ground now! Without the energy you need for eating and digesting there's a lot more left for observation and communication. Muriel and I have noticed this in particular, and this is just day two! It seems to be going more slowly with Petrus and Elisabeth but Maruko says it has to do with how many toxins and how much negative energy you have to let go of, so it takes longer for some people than others. But he said too that Muriel and I are probably more the exception than the rule because it takes longer with people who have less experience with meditation and are less open to things! And fortunately Petrus and Elisabeth still have enough time over the next seven days to reach this level; we will support each other unconditionally for this of course, even with all the resistance involved. The nine days are designed to work for everyone so we have full confidence. To sum up, we are all inspired and looking forward to the three days without food and drink to come!

Melodie van Hellingen

17th September 2016
Day 6

The sixth day already! The past three days were very special, with day five, right in the middle of the process, as the high point. Already on day four all 4 of us were very quiet and relaxed. I began to feel some kind of vibrations myself and to see all kinds of moving little dots, very special. I think I was the only one who saw them. But it had a clear effect on all of us. We are getting closer to our feelings and all the external stuff, our masks, are falling away. This has released intense emotions, particularly in Petrus. He had so much resistance today that he threatened to abandon the process and even leave the group! But by talking it all through, and with Muriel's help, I was able to have him see that it is precisely these strong emotions which show how much he needs this process and our group to move away from his own solitude. In the end he suffered a serious attack, which felt threatening to all three of us, but once all the emotions were finally released, they were replaced by a deep calm. It felt like a genuine liberation—for Petrus himself, but also for me and for Muriel. Conflict and love turn out to be two sides of the same coin and everything leads to a much deeper unity in the end. Very grateful to be experiencing this beautiful journey with the four of us and the others in America.

Melodie van Hellingen

20th September 2016
Day 9

Rounded off the process this afternoon with the nine-day group. We feel reborn as a group but also each of us personally. Fantastic to be able to look back on such an intense and freeing period! Food turns out to be a massively addictive and distracting factor in our lives, even more than we had thought. Now we have freed ourselves of it, we can choose how big we want food's role in our lives to be. This gives a great deal of energy to be able to concentrate on the really important things: personal development and growth and genuine contact, feeling what you need and then, from that setting, bringing a different narrative (and a different SOUND!) into the world, for more harmony (LOVE!), and a more natural and sustainable lifestyle without damaging the earth. We're really looking forward to living without dependence on food. And we'd recommend the nine-day process to anyone!

P.S. Click on this link for a recording of the "We are light" affirmations which I set to music (if you listen carefully you might recognize the tune of the "Three Times Table" song, which I've given a more spiritual interpretation.)

Liesbeth clicks on the link and a YouTube video appears on her screen and automatically begins to play. Photos of the housemates glide across the screen, accompanied by shaky *a cappella* singing. She does indeed recognize the old school song for the three times table, with here and there an extra note added to make the lyrics fit the music. When the film has finished, a new one starts up. *Introducing the members of the Sound & Love Commune!* is written in coloured letters, and one by one the four inhabitants appear on the screen and introduce themselves.

Even before the film has finished, Liesbeth clicks on repeat. She moves the red ball under the images with her cursor to the moment that Elisabeth appears, the last of the four, to tell something about herself. It's one sentence, pronounced with difficulty. Liesbeth plays the fragment a few times in succession, allowing Elisabeth to speak to her through her computer's speakers.

"I'm Elisabeth and I'm Melodie's sister."

"I'm Elisabeth and I'm Melodie's sister."

"I'm Elisabeth and I'm Melodie's sister."

16

We are doubts. Muriel managed to keep us hidden away for a very long time and act as though we weren't there, but since she's been arrested and placed all on her own in a closed space of just seven cubic metres, she's found it more and more difficult to ignore us. But now she's in the small interview room, with her lawyer sitting diagonally behind her, and Liesbeth and Asif, who are both trying to put on their kindest faces, across from her, ready to feed us with confusing facts and questions, we hope it won't be too long before we win out.

"The fact is we received the forensic pathologist's report yesterday," Asif says. "And it concludes that your housemate died of malnutrition."

"And you just said you thought everyone started feeling better after you'd gone through the nine-day process together," Liesbeth adds, "but perhaps you can have a think, now you know that malnutrition caused her death, whether you might remember certain things. Things that might have suggested that Elisabeth wasn't doing so well. Mainly in terms of her health."

"Her health," Muriel repeats.

"Yes," Asif says. "Small things maybe. Signs of weakness. Loss of stamina. Hair loss. Weight loss.

Skin problems. If you look back now, can you remember any times when you noticed anything like that?"

And with this question we can finally move from the concealed part of Muriel's consciousness to the accessible part, making room for the thought that the answer may be yes, that there was a reason she herself could never sleep from the hunger, that there was a reason she lay awake adding up her own calorie intake and that of the others, a reason the results of those sums had made her stomach hurt even more over recent weeks, and that Elisabeth was indeed the person she had been most worried about. And as openhearted as Muriel is, just as she's about to share this realization with the detectives she remembers why she's here, that she's a suspect and that her lawyer had told her that if she had any doubts about whether to tell them something because it was potentially incriminating, always ask for a break so they could confer. She looks back at her lawyer who gives her a friendly nod.

"I'd like to talk to my lawyer in private please."

Asif and Liesbeth exchange a glance, nod at her lawyer, and get to their feet. As soon as they've left the room, the lawyer moves his chair forward so that he's sitting next to her, and with a concerned look in his eyes—a bit like her father, Muriel thinks—he asks what the matter is.

"Tell me," he says, "tell me, lass," and for a moment his regional accent is audible, reminding Muriel even more of her father, and tears shoot into her eyes, but he doesn't give her the chance to burst into tears. "Tell me as quickly and concisely as you can."

Muriel nods, swallows a couple of times, and begins to talk. All of the memories, big and small, and thoughts that have awoken us over the past days rise to the surface. Since she underwent the nine-day process two years ago, Muriel realizes she has actually suffered from constant hunger. Perhaps they all didn't feel better but were instead in some kind of a daze, perhaps she had a kind of fog in her head the whole time that stopped her from being able to think properly—which was certainly pleasant in one way but perhaps it had been a sign that what they'd been doing wasn't entirely healthy, and she was the one who usually repaired their clothes and she'd had to take in all their trousers a few times, Elisabeth's even more often, which had also made her wonder whether they were doing it well enough and whether Elisabeth in particular could cope, because the man from the nine-day process wasn't that thin at all, he even had a bit of a belly, if her eyes hadn't been deceiving her, while all four of them in the house had lost weight, and without wanting to accuse Melodie, she suspected, looking back, that Melodie was the only one who showed true enthusiasm, and Melodie is a person who is very good at inspiring others with her enthusiasm, a person who gives you the feeling you can trust them, she simply knows a lot, she's really wise because of everything she's experienced herself, and then it's difficult sometimes to disagree with her, so if she says, or said, that she felt it was very liberating for everyone and that you could hear their voices were purer when they sang, you were inclined to believe it, because Melodie is also the one who knows the most about music, and she has perfect pitch, but when Muriel looks back now, she does wonder whether she ever felt truly liberated, like a butterfly, she means, one that could spread its wings and fly away at any moment, and she thinks she didn't; it was more like everything became more time-consuming and complicated, because all in all it took up quite a lot of time, singing the affirmations, doing the breathing and light sessions, and also the conversations about how it affected you and the discussions about when they'd eat again and how to handle being offered food by someone, and Melodie spent a lot of time on newsletters and Facebook posts where she wrote about not eating, and sometimes Muriel even got the idea that it was a way of saving money, because all their recent subsidy applications had been turned down, and once again she doesn't want to speak ill of Melodie but to return to the officers' question about their health, it had been incredibly tough physically the last weeks, for everyone in fact, because they'd spent a lot of time indoors at home and now they suddenly had to travel to Melodie's mother every day, who lived in a different city, and Muriel had calculated one sleepless night that you'd burn at least 500 kilocalories extra a day doing this, while they weren't drinking any more vegetable juice, so if you went on the assumption that they weren't entirely capable of living on light and air but needed the energy they got through nutrition, then it had been a period in which they'd used a lot more energy, while before that time they'd also repeatedly consumed too little, and to return again to the detectives' question, she had noticed last week that Elisabeth couldn't keep up at all, literally, because a few times on a walk with Melodie's mother—and Elisabeth's too, Elisabeth and Melodie's mother—she'd sat down on the curb because she couldn't go any further, and they'd all waited for her to regain her breath and Melodie had helped her up again and they could walk on, but in retrospect this didn't seem entirely healthy to Muriel, and to return even more specifically to the question of whether there had been any signs that Elisabeth wasn't well, she thinks in retrospect that the answer is yes, she thinks that she may even have said something that night, though she's no longer entirely sure, whether she said it or just thought it, but she is certain she did wonder whether they shouldn't call a doctor, or the emergency services, and she isn't entirely sure, if she did say it, whether Melodie actually replied that it wasn't necessary because what was happening was natural, or whether she only thought that Melodie would *probably* say this so that she decided not to ask the question about the doctor and the ambulance, but whatever the case, immediately after that she had agreed entirely with Melodie that it was very natural and right that Elisabeth had died, and it is only now looking back she has started to have her doubts, about everything in fact, about whether not eating is possible or not, and whether everything that is natural is automatically better, and whether she became happier after she moved into the Sound & Love Commune, and many more things, but the most painful and dangerous of those doubts is whether it isn't her fault that Elisabeth died, because she didn't call an ambulance, even though she did think about it and maybe even said it out loud, because if she had called, then Elisabeth might still be alive now, and they might have been able to get a more realistic picture of the effects of light nutrition on their health, because perhaps they would have to conclude that they weren't simply ready for it yet, spiritually speaking; Melodie was, of course, but Muriel still needs food, to be honest, in any case she feels a little better now after eating those sandwiches, but if she tells all of this to the police—she gulps a few times more—then she might have to go to prison, and she's not sure she can do that, be alone for so long, and it would be terrible to have to tell her parents, even though she actually doesn't talk to them anymore, but she's realized that she'd like to change that, she'd like to see whether she could meet with her family again sometimes, but even if she doesn't tell them herself and they hear of it, then it would still be an enormous shock and disappointment for them that the girl who had always shown so much promise had been convicted of the manslaughter of her housemate, this would really disappoint and hurt her father, and her mother probably too, and she doesn't want this, she wants to prevent it if she can, but she doesn't want to break the law and lie to the police, and she wants to say more but her lawyer interrupts her, there isn't enough time to talk much longer, he says, so the remaining two minutes would be best spent on going through their strategy for the questioning. He's the type of person we can barely get a grip of, someone who always seems certain of how things work, who has to fall into a profound crisis before we can get a hold of him, and now too he knows exactly what has to happen: Muriel has to keep everything she's just told him to herself. Of course you mustn't lie when you are being questioned, Muriel's right about that, but you can only speak the truth about things you know for sure, he tells her, so if she isn't sure about what she said or thought about calling an ambulance or doctor, then it's best to say nothing. And, as for the rest, he proposes they give as superficial answers as they can.

"Repeat after me," he says. "If there were signs, then I didn't notice them at the time."

"If there were signs, then I didn't notice them at the time."

"Excellent. One more time."

"If there were signs, then I didn't notice them at the time."

"Very good. And if they ask if there were signs, just say: I no longer remember. Because you do no longer remember. What you remember now, you are interpreting retrospectively as signs, but that wasn't the case at the moment they happened. You believed Melodie too, didn't you? You believed you were all doing the right thing?"

Muriel nods slowly.

"Well then. So you can just say you don't remember any alarming signs because you no longer know whether they alarmed you, and if you say it like that, it's definitely not lying."

Again Muriel nods, now with less hesitation. We have to give it to him: it seems he has managed to twist us in such a way that we make Muriel seem less rather than more guilty, by making her doubt all the incriminating facts she has just admitted to him. To give her a final push before the officers come back in, he says, "Because you don't want to be imprisoned for any longer, and that's very understandable because you don't belong here, that's one thing that is certain. So just remember this: you don't remember any signs of weakness or other alarming signals."

And Muriel, who is used to doing what other people tell her with conviction, does what her lawyer says. When Asif and Liesbeth come back in and pick up the conversation again, she repeats the line she has practised and represses the question of whether what she is saying is true, whether it wasn't different, after all, and she manages this easily too: she knows how to repress us in favour of one clear narrative she can believe in.

The more often Muriel repeats her lines, the glummer Asif and Liesbeth look. Her lawyer listens with a condescending smile, clearly thrilled with his tactic to have Muriel believe in her own semi-true statement. She does fantastically, not letting anything slip that the police might use against her. He watches calmly as Asif and Liesbeth work Muriel, he with an increasingly forced, friendly tone of inquiry, she with her arms folded more and more tightly, until the two of them give up and end the questioning. With the feeling that she has escaped by the skin of her teeth, Muriel lets herself be led back to her cell and we go with her, ready to pounce once she is alone again.

17

We are the story. Slowly and predictably we head toward our conclusion—climax or anti-climax, it remains to be seen. We suspect it's going to be an anti-climax, if the writer carries on this way. We long for a good push, an unexpected twist, a new character who knows things that put everything that has gone before in a different light, but it seems the writer has other things on her mind. Her stomach ache and the accompanying medical diagnoses she finds on the internet are more important to her than her characters, our characters, who are dangling in the void right now like forgotten marionettes, waiting to be set in motion again. The writer doesn't have time to invent things that would make us more interesting, not while there's still so much exciting stuff to be told.

Stuff about Elisabeth, for example, about what had made her so instable, and why she spoke so little that the outside world took her to be simpleminded. It makes us think there must have been more to it, that it must be possible to think up a cause. Incest maybe, or that she was abused by the boy next door. Or maybe she was bullied as a child, things like that can lead to compelling scenes. Or it could have gone wrong even earlier. Perhaps, before she had Elisabeth, her mother had an abortion and felt guilty toward the other child she lost, which led her to more or less ignore Elisabeth after she was born, or maybe even before that, which could be described with a hospital scene just after the birth where the mother almost forgets to take her daughter home with her, which might suggest that Elisabeth had become invisible to the people around her from birth, and remained so, until she literally disappeared.

Or, what could be a nice addition—something about asking for help. Say that somewhere over the coming pages it turns out that just before Elisabeth died she'd asked for help. She could have said, in a weak voice—that to make it even more pitiful could only be understood by Melodie, for example— "Help me, help me"; or something more specific, "Cola, give me some cola." Just a suggestion. Coca Cola might not be quite the right fit for Elisabeth, but on the other hand who knows what a person thinks when they're on the verge of death? If she did her best, she could make it quite convincing, our writer. Otherwise, she could turn the coke into juice. Or elderflower cordial. "Give me some elderflower cordial." Or she could write that Elisabeth asked for a doctor and Petrus had picked up the phone but Melodie stopped him and they had a row, a row that Melodie won because she claimed that the fact Petrus wanted to call the doctor was a form of flight, which always worked well because Petrus never wanted to be the kind of person who fled, but first he had screamed his head off before agreeing with Melodie, which gave her ammunition, because look at what you're doing, Petrus, you're standing there screaming while Elisabeth lies here critically ill, this is unacceptable, this behaviour is not okay—you're okay, Petrus, I'll never reject you as a person, but this is unacceptable, are you feeling better now, are you able to calm down a bit, go and sit down on the couch and take a deep breath. Something like that would be good, that there was a big row that nobody knows about, not the police either, and that it comes to light right at the end of Melodie's interrogation, who suddenly breaks due to an empathetic comment from Asif that strikes home, and then she tells this whole untold episode to the detectives just like that.

And something else the writer could do, she could give us a clearer picture of that Maruko, the man from the nine-day process, a dedicated preacher of harmful ideas, by describing for example how Melodie had asked him during the video call whether it was true that *everyone* was capable of letting go of food because not everyone she lived with was equally healthy, and neither were they equally advanced in terms of spiritual development, and some of them were experiencing some mental resistance, to which Maruko had replied that he was sure everyone could do it, and it didn't have to do with physical strength so much as with persistence, so it was important that she, the person who had asked the question, *Melodie, what a beautiful name by the way, it suits you so well,* continued to believe in the path they were taking so that she could help her friends to persevere because ultimately they would all grow. Something like that.

Though we have to say that by now we are starting to get a bit fed up with all the attention focused on

Melodie. Every time we start to move in Elisabeth's direction, Melodie gets in the way. The writer—who could better understand their intentions than us— wants to make it appear like Elisabeth is a big mystery that cannot be solved, a black hole that can only be perceived through the movement of everything around it. She wants to leave the mystery of Elisabeth intact, because this is what she thinks real life is like, that other people, particularly those who are dead, are mysteries that, to our frustration, cannot be solved, but we don't really understand why she needed to abuse us to demonstrate this point. Because what do you think? Real life? As if we resemble real life. Have you ever seen a story that starts talking in real life? So why should we leave mysteries intact simply because there are mysteries in real life? There are enough stories that don't shy away from giving suitable explanations for things that happen. Detective stories for example, in which all the relevant motives and entanglements are laid bare at the end. Stories with real murders and murderers. But no, up to now the writer has deliberately kept us unsatisfying and ambiguous. And this doesn't help us as a story, certainly not in combination with you, the reader, because intentionally or unintentionally you are just as guilty of lack of clarity as the writer. How often have you thought about other things while you were reading? And how often have you read into us things that weren't there at all? Between the lines, certainly. All the effort we've gone to in order to remain ourselves, despite all the ambiguity the writer has saddled us with, and then you go and turn it into something else inside your head, a poor reproduction, full of gaps and incorrect assumptions and interpretations. And don't think you're not one of those readers. Go on, turn back to page 17 and read out loud—yes, out loud, because you read more carefully that way— what it says there. Had you remembered it exactly the way it was written down? We don't think so. If you truly want to do us justice, you'll have to read the whole thing out loud, as slowly as possible, running your finger over the words you are reading so that you don't miss anything. But you won't have time for that. No time. As though we aren't busy, with everything that's going on.

But fine, maybe we're too strict. Despite everything, you have persevered with us to this point and that's something you have going for you. Off the record, compared to the average reader, you've been one of the more attentive ones. And more important than rereading is reading on so that we can at least reach our conclusion in your mind, even if that conclusion might not be entirely satisfying. We'll just tell you now to avoid disappointment: we won't unfold very differently from what you are already expecting.

Muriel, who is confused about her responsibility for Elisabeth's death, and has started to question whether stopping eating was actually good for her—which begs the question of whether the commune is the right place for her—will flirt with the idea of leaving the group, but at the present time it doesn't look like she actually will. The kind of loyalty she feels to the others can't be shattered by a few days in a police station, and if you add to that the fact that her social contacts outside the group have been reduced to zilch, it would be very odd if she did dare to leave. Perhaps she'll believe for a while that she does dare, but once she's released—and they'll be released tomorrow, you don't have to worry about that, this isn't the type of crime, if it is a crime, for which people are detained for weeks, and in any case there isn't much evidence; it's quite tragic, but on the scale of bad things that can happen in the world it's not that bad, no real murder has been committed, as we already noted with regret—once they are released and can talk to each other, we don't think there's much chance that Muriel will really be able to break free, because right now Melodie is the only person she's got, and Muriel is the type who needs other people to be able to stay afloat. She hasn't been in touch with the two other people who could help her—her parents—in two years, and her guilt about this episode with Elisabeth will make it extra hard for her to face them, so the chance she'll leave the group seems negligible to us. The same goes for Petrus, who was prompted by the police's questions and by taking up smoking again to look at things differently. He did wonder for a moment whether Melodie hadn't got everything wrong, and over the coming hours he will certainly spend time thinking about that as he lies on the bed in his cell fighting with himself and trying to sleep, but he will finally come to the conclusion that Melodie is the only one who accepts him the way he is, the only one who can help him break free of his habits. And where Melodie is concerned, she won't crack during her interrogation and tell the detectives any untold episode but will stubbornly stick to her own half truths about the night of Elisabeth's death.

And then we've got the detectives, who aside from being detectives are also real people with their own personal problems related to the case—in this way we do resemble an English detective series on TV, but as far as we're concerned that part could have been left out, now that the substantial elements of a good crime story are lacking, such as a serious crime and the promise of a decisive answer as to who did it—in any case, the detectives will fail to discover or deduce anything else of significance. So, our conclusion will be that varying circumstances led to the ill-fated plan to stop eating, which turned out to be fatal to the oldest and weakest inhabitant of the commune, but that this isn't enough to prosecute her housemates, and for the housemates themselves, facing up to their own roles in Elisabeth's death is too painful, so they will carry on with their lives no wiser, and who knows, perhaps there will be some reflection on the dynamics between the characters and the way in which those dynamics amplified their individual blindness, because it's particularly difficult for Melodie to admit that the path she chose cost her own sister her life, while Muriel's obsession with sums might have saved Elisabeth if Muriel had taken her obsession more seriously, and more such considerations that finally all come down to "if this had happened, that would have happened," but if *ifs* and *ands* were pots and pans, it still wouldn't change our ending. The forensic pathologist won't suddenly discover that Elisabeth died of a totally different cause, something her senile mother might have had a hand in, or that in a fit of madness Muriel cleaned the slow juicer with bleach, accidentally poisoning Elisabeth, or that right at the end Melodie held the pillow over Elisabeth's face to put her out of her misery more quickly; we don't expect anything like that, we haven't been that kind of story so far, so we won't suddenly turn into one. You'll have to make do with detailed descriptions of their last day in custody, and what happens after that when they get home. Which we've already told you: nothing special. They'll just go home and their lives will carry on. But if you don't mind reading about thoughts and events that are barely worth mentioning, as you clearly have done up to now without much reluctance, then we'd appreciate it if you'd read on. Though we would like to impress upon you to read more attentively from this point on so that you distort us as little as possible in your mind. "Read out loud" is our motto, because reading out loud makes you read more carefully, let's repeat it one more time, because by now you have probably already forgotten.

18

We are senile dementia. We are proof that a person is not the same as what they can remember and understand. Look at this person, what's-its-name, her name, Jannetje, Jansje, Hansje, Hansje. Only because she didn't recognize the man who just came in, an older man, white hair, worried expression, somewhere between angry and sad, only because she doesn't know who he is, which doesn't mean to say that she's no longer herself, maybe she's more herself, who's to say, not us, and not Hansje either, and not this man, he must be a relative of hers or something, or yes, her husband probably because he kisses her on the lips and without knowing why she kisses him back because the movement is still in her lips, and out of her mouth come the words "Hello love" because those words sound nice along with the movement of the kiss, and also the words "Nice that you're here, lovely to see you," and then there's a moment of silence as the man pulls up a chair, he moves it so that he can sit facing her, and he does this too, he sits down, their knees almost touch and his face is still so ... so worried, probably his memory bothering him, there is something he's remembered and that he's worrying about now, and what it is is the name of a woman, he says the name, he says, "It's Elisabeth," and Hansje tries to copy the sounds and manages wonderfully, "Elisabeth," it sounds familiar, Elisabeth, what could be wrong with this Elisabeth, the name reminds us of something, maybe it's one of the women who come here often, visiting, women who know her well, family members, daughters perhaps, there's a man too, there are four of them and maybe one of the four is called Elisabeth, that's quite possible, maybe it's the one who always walks next to her when they go for a stroll, that's her daughter, yes, must be because she always calls her "Mum," the other day when they were leaving, after they'd put Hansje to bed, they always do that, then Hansje doesn't have to wait for the ladies, then she can go to sleep early, which is nice, the other day, one of the women kissed her and said "Bye, Mum," and Hansje echoed, "Bye bye," and the woman said "Night night, sleep tight," and in response Hansje opened her arms and said to the other three, perhaps family too, perhaps not, maybe in-laws or something else, who were standing next to her bed waiting for the woman who had said goodnight, "Do I get a kiss then?" and yes yes yes, then we heard the name Elisabeth, the woman said "Hey, did you hear that, Elisabeth, Mum wants you to give her a kiss," she said that to the other woman, Elisabeth, who didn't say goodnight but stood there waiting, and who carried on standing there afterwards, but the goodnight woman said "Go on, Elisabeth, give Mum a kiss," Elisabeth yes, that's what she said again then, and then the other woman knelt by her bed and kissed Hansje on the cheek and she said, Hansje, not the woman, Hansje herself said "Bye darling, sleep well, won't you?" which felt good in her mouth, in Hansje's mouth, and she wrapped her arms tightly around the woman and held her, for a moment, so this probably was Elisabeth, who didn't speak herself but carried on waiting as Hansje hugged her, waiting for Hansje to let go of her, but first Hansje said "sleep well" again and only then did she let go and the woman got up and patted down her clothes, which hadn't got dirty from the hug, we thought, and then the other woman said Elisabeth again, she said "This is very special. Wonderful, Elisabeth. Beautiful the way you are opening yourself up. And Mum too, she genuinely felt that. It shows that she's not senile at all, not like everyone says," and the woman who'd patted her clothing nodded and they went away, all three of the women and the man, so one of them might have been called Elisabeth, and that's why the name sounds familiar to us, the name the man just said, not the man who came with the women, that was a different man, he didn't have white hair, but this man, the man who just arrived, and now he's saying some more words and another name, "Last night Melodie called me, she couldn't talk for long because the police were there, all she could say was that Elisabeth—I'm sorry, but Elisabeth is dead," he says and takes hold of Hansje's hands and that is better because the words are too much to understand in one go, *Elisabeth, called, police, dead*, too many words to understand, even though we are living proof that a person isn't the same as their ability to understand all the words they used to understand, she only has to understand one or two, in fact, and then not even to know the exact meaning of them, if she gets the gist, and also helpful in this is the way the man, her husband probably, holds her hands and looks at her with watery eyes, because she feels her own eyes tear up now and she replies in an appropriate tone, "Oh. Dead. She died. What, oh," and this is exactly what the man wants to hear because he nods and says "Yes, yes, you do understand, don't you, what that means? Our daughter," and now some tears come too, from his eyes, and he clutches her hands a little tighter and says "Still our daughter, isn't she, despite everything," and what does it matter that she no longer remembers exactly what daughter means, it's more about the big picture, and even without the details she is able to join in crying over the name, Elisabeth—was that her daughter, had he just said that, that it was her daughter—with the man who is holding her hands, even without understanding what he is saying about detention and police and we don't know for how long and Johan says and Johan asked and Johan offered if necessary and arrange the funeral and wait and not much chance and think about it and look back and we did do our best and you too you always did your best and I really appreciate that and not too strict and Johan says and nonsense and I do sometimes wonder and this might sound crazy and actually quite happy and arrest and see the errors of their ways and housemates and but this is a cruel price to pay and Melodie and not the fault of and but and Johan did think and Melodie has the right or shouldn't it be us and buried and wait and Johan called and body is usually only released and not start a new fight and enough to deal with and fortunately and sorry that and bother and the nurses and inform and well and sorry state of affairs and whatever and wait and very sad and daughter and loss and it isn't right and parent and outlives child and also for you and spent a lot of time with you and Melodie and email and last week and you and Elisabeth and that you spontaneously gave her a hug and didn't think and last time and parting and still a nice thought and well and comforting and don't you think; what does it matter if Hansje doesn't exactly understand or doesn't understand at all what those words are, as long as she understands his intention, and she understands that he means something that goes with a serious expression and she nods at everything he says and when he stops talking she says "Yes, yes" and sometimes she repeats a few words, "Really comforting yes," and then suddenly on an impulse, because her arms seem to want to, she takes his face in her hands and pulls it to her and presses her lips to the top of his white head and she says "Really comforting, you're right, hush now, hush now," and they remain sitting like this for a while, until the man carefully takes her hands and puts them back in her lap and sits up straight and says "You'll manage here, won't you? This is a good place for you. Better. Better than at home, right? For both of us," and she says "yes" and "better" and he likes to hear that, it reassures him apparently, and then he asks "Shall I read the letters to the editor to you?" and without waiting for an answer, he gets a newspaper out of his bag and begins to read out loud, and Hansje's head moves along to the rhythm of the words, up and down, up and down, until her chin sinks to her chest and her breathing becomes heavier and when the man has finished reading and looks up he nods and folds up the paper again and quietly slides it back into his bag, and he gets a cloth out of his trouser pocket which he first uses to wipe his eyes and then very quietly, so that she doesn't wake up, blows his nose, then he carefully slides back the chair he was sitting on and stands up, he gives her another kiss on her head and walks away, and that is nice for her, that the man who came to visit, it was her husband, we thought, that he allows her to sleep when she's tired, and that he is able to think it is better for her here than at home, and perhaps that is the case, because there aren't any ladies to do things for her at home, such as put things in her mouth that she has to swallow and poke needles in her arm, things that don't always feel nice, but unfortunately they have to happen the ladies say, and just take a few more sips, yes it is a bit bitter isn't it, but nearly all gone, good girl, and now this one with a glass of water, drink it up, and that's nice of the ladies and also them putting nappies on her so she doesn't have to get out of her bed or her chair to pee or poo, she can just stay sitting or lying there and let it all go, now too, now too, now she's dozing in her chair and is momentarily alarmed because she feels the urge to pee, and she looks around searchingly because just now there was a man, the man, the sweet man, he was the love, she can still feel that word in her mouth and now she tries to stand up to look for him after she's had a pee, but what is that place actually, that place where people always do that, and how is she going to get up, one two, one two, no, again, a two, and for a moment her bottom comes free from the seat but then she falls back down again, "Hey, hey, hey?" she asks out loud and then one of those ladies come to her, "Are you alright, Mrs Van Hellingen?" and Hansje says "Hey," she wants to say something else, something to make it more clear that she wants to go to that place, but all that comes out of her mouth is "Hey" and "Yes" and the lady asks "What do you want?" and Hansje moves her upper body back and forth and then the words come, "I want to go to that place," and the lady asks, "Do you need to pee?" "Yes, yes, pee," Hansje says and the lady says "You can pee, it's not a problem, you're wearing a nappy. Just pee. The nappy will catch it. We'll change it this evening," and that's nice, that the lady says Hansje is allowed to stay sitting there, and as she pees she feels the warmth between her legs, nice and warm, yes, but where is the man, the love, he was still here just now, and now he's gone, maybe gone home, maybe she should go home too, but the ladies have just cooked dinner and then it isn't polite to suddenly leave, and after dinner they've come to help her they say, they help her to a bed and they undress her, they just do this, why not, and then they change her nappy and say goodnight, which is very sweet of them, and it's nice and warm, the thing doesn't work, the thing that makes it cold, but maybe it will tomorrow, and better too hot than too cold, but something isn't right because first there was a man and there was a name too, Elisabeth, and there were tears too and now there are new tears, out of the blue it seems, and Hansje sobs and sobs and sobs until a lady comes to check on her and says "Aw. Are you sad? Yes. Good reason too. She was your daughter, after all," and the lady squeezes Hansje's hand and gets something white to wipe away the snot that is dripping down Hansje's top lip, and then she puts the white thing over her nose and says "Have a good blow, have a good blow," and the connection between the word *blow* and the feeling of the white thing on her nose still works, Hansje blows and the rest of the snot comes out, and her nose is dry again and that's sweet of the lady, they are all sweet ladies here, and maybe there was something that wasn't quite right just now but what was it again

19

We are goat-wool socks, hand-knitted by Hansje, Melodie's mother, when she was still mentally capable of knitting socks. It must have been about five or so years ago. Holes have appeared in our heels but Melodie still likes to wear us, so fortunately she happened to be wearing us the evening Elisabeth died. At least she had two soft and familiar items of clothing on her chilly feet for all the horrible things that have happened to her since. Not that it's really cold—it's even on the hot side in the cell where she has to sleep—but Melodie's circulation has always been quite poor, and eating so little these days hasn't improved things. She hasn't eaten anything at all since she got to the police station because she doesn't trust the food here. And of course she is in shock. Her sister dead, herself arrested and separated from her housemates, and all of it so sudden. Things like that really affect a sensitive person such as Melodie.

The day before it all happened we went on a nice afternoon walk in the park behind Hansje's nursing home.

"Look, Mum," Melodie had said, "I'm wearing your socks." They'd stopped at a bench because Elisabeth wanted to rest a while. Melodie stood in front of her mother's wheelchair and pulled her trouser legs up a bit. "You knitted these, can you remember? You were always so good at knitting."

"Oh yes," Hansje replied. "Yes." She smiled and nodded.

"They're still lovely and warm."

"Yes. Lovely, my child. Lovely."

"Mum is always happy when I wear her socks," Melodie said to no one in particular, letting her trouser legs fall back down. "Are you alright, Elisabeth? Shall we carry on? Otherwise it's so boring for Mum." She went over to Elisabeth to help her to her feet and gave her an arm. "Come on, it's not much further. Do you still have those socks of Mum's?"

"I don't think so," Elisabeth replies.

"Too bad."

This was the afternoon, and in the evening Elisabeth lay down on the sofa and said she couldn't carry on, and a few hours later she died and now we're here at the police station, been here for a couple of days already, and Melodie is sitting at a table, her toes curled, in a small, cheerless room, with a couple of other people whom we don't know very well: a man and a woman who ask her questions, and a woman called Rose, that's her lawyer, she's sitting behind Melodie on a chair with its back to the wall, a very nice woman that, she gave Melodie a lot of comfort the first morning she arrived here.

Melodie's feet are a bit sweaty, probably because she's a bit nervous, and we are hoping the way we envelop her feet reassures her, with all the softness and warmth and love that her mother put into us when she made us. Her mother, who would say to

Melodie at moments like this that all those nerves are uncalled for, because she's fine the way she is, and also because most people really do mean well, even the man and the woman who are asking questions; they come across as very friendly, very interested in Melodie, and in Elisabeth too. Very dedicated, particularly the woman. It's as though she retrospectively wants to save Elisabeth. And both of them are good listeners; they're very quiet when Melodie is talking and as soon as she's finished they neatly summarize what she's just said.

They ask her about the turning point, they want to know whether Melodie can identify a turning point. A moment when "Elisabeth's condition," as the woman calls it, became life-threatening.

Of course, we are only socks and death isn't our specialty, but if you asked us the question, we'd say: when the four of them got back from the nursing home. As soon as they were inside, Elisabeth said "I can't go on. I'm done," and went to lie down on the sofa without saying anything more, after which she immediately lost consciousness.

At least that's what we'd say, that she was unconscious. Melodie is still talking in a very well-intended way about sleep, but we think her sister was unconscious, because she didn't wake up again, not even when Melodie and the others laid her on the airbed, and that wasn't an easy procedure, a sleeping person really would have been woken up by that. But Melodie continues to clamp onto the word *sleep*. Maybe because *unconscious* sounds too hard to her. Melodie is very sensitive to direct language, especially when it refers to people she loves. She continues to be riled by the word *dementia* for example. She'd rather that *confused* or *impaired* were used. Otherwise it's simply too overwhelming for her. And she already has so much to bear with the emotional ups and downs of her housemates. Actually, those housemates are too much for her, we sometimes think, with her hypersensitivity to things, but she's simply one of those people who likes to play a significant role in other people's lives.

"We didn't think it was a good idea to wake her up. She was so tired," is what Melodie says then, and the woman asking the question—very dedicated she seems to us, definitely that, but also a bit strict—now wants to know which of them exactly thought that waking her up, or checking whether Elisabeth was conscious, wasn't necessary, and whether the three of them had discussed it.

"All three of us thought it wasn't necessary," Melodie says, curling her toes even tighter. "We've been living together for years. A lot of the time we don't need words to understand each other. All three of us felt very clearly that Elisabeth wanted to sleep. I felt it myself and I felt that the others felt it too, so it was logical for us to be quiet and let her sleep."

Don't get us wrong, we really love Melodie. We couldn't wish for a better mission in life than to keep her feet warm. But we don't quite understand why she is so imprecise when she talks about things we experienced with her. Now, for example, now she's saying they were all quiet and let Elisabeth sleep, and here she is not being entirely accurate because after Elisabeth had lain down on the sofa, Muriel did begin to speak, we thought. "Shouldn't w—" she said, if we heard correctly, but Melodie seemed to want her to keep quiet, probably in part because of the brutality of the word *shouldn't*, because we heard her say *shhhh* quite emphatically and after that Muriel shut up. So yes, ultimately they were quiet, but the way we remember it, it wasn't logical for all three of them, in any case not for Muriel. Although perhaps Melodie remembers things differently, because Melodie is a real lover of harmony, so much so that she often forgets arguments and disagreements as fast as she can.

"And when you laid her on the airbed, how did she react then? Can you describe it?"

"She wasn't very comfortable on the sofa," Melodie says, "with her head half against the armrest, that wasn't nice for her neck, so we thought it would be better to put her on the airbed."

"And how did that go? What was said? Who did what?"

Melodie stretches her toes and presses them to the floor. "It went very organically, in fact. I thought I'd already told you and I don't understand why you are asking about it again. I don't understand why you are being so aggressive. We are the only people who were always there for her, who always helped her, however difficult she sometimes was, because my sister really wasn't always that easy. So if you act like we did something to my sister, while all we did was lay her in bed with total loving care, it comes across as very hurtful, after everything I did for her."

"We're not suggesting anything," the strict, dedicated woman says. "We're only asking questions. We want to know as precisely as possible what happened.

Which includes the way you laid her on the airbed. Organically, you said. But what does that mean? Who did what? Who said what? Whose idea was it? Who fetched the airbed? Try to take us along with you in your organic process." The irritation in her voice doesn't escape us, nor Melodie, of course, with her sensitivity. She presses her heels into the floor, and then we hear a different voice, a very friendly female voice behind Melodie, an angel of sorts it seems, but it is Rose, the lawyer, and Rose says to Melodie that she can simply give a calm factual answer to the question, indeed in as much as she remembers everything, and at this Melodie relaxes her feet a little, and a little more calmly than just before, she describes how they laid Elisabeth in bed, for the main part sticking to the facts as we experienced them. She stood near her head and Petrus was at the other end, near Elizabeth's feet. In the meantime, Muriel put down the mattress. When they were moving her, Melodie was checking Elisabeth's face the whole time, she says, and the strict lady asks if she didn't find it concerning or strange that Elisabeth didn't wake up, and she says she didn't, because Elisabeth was very tired, and because Melodie didn't have any other reasons to think her sister might be in danger. And she still doesn't think Elisabeth was in danger now, for that matter, because to her it is clear that Elisabeth was ready to take the next step. It was a liberation for her.

"So you are claiming that you did foresee her death but that you didn't see it as a danger?"

"No," says Melodie, "no, I think it's terrible, you saying it like that, that I foresaw it. It was a process, she was tired, she wanted to rest, that's what we saw. And that rest slowly deepened. We didn't know where it was going, we only saw the process, and in the end she found the ultimate place of rest. Why should we hold someone back if they're in that kind of process?"

"And did you speak to each other about this? I mean, are you certain that your housemates thought about it in the same way?"

"I've told you that we are of the same mind. Definitely when something deep is happening. Then you don't need words, you just understand each other."

"Alright," says the man, who hasn't asked much up to now. "So to be very concrete: none of you said out loud that your sister as you formulated it 'was ready to take the next step.' And you didn't discuss the fact that it was better not to intervene. But as you experienced it, what was happening was good and you weren't worried that she might die, because you didn't see death as dangerous. Can you then conclude that you understood she would die, but still decided not to intervene?"

"What do you mean, intervene? Why would you intervene in a natural process? A life that wants to end should be allowed to end. A body that is spent is spent."

"A body that isn't fed fails, yes," the woman opposite her comments, again with a sharp edge to her voice. "But in general we don't call that natural. If after a long period of eating far too little a person displays these signs, you could call it a natural process but you could also ask yourself whether that person might not be better off eating something, and whether they might need help to be able to regain their strength. Allowing a person who is exhausted to die, at that age, and with that diet, is not the only possibility." Her voice grows increasingly loud, she sounds genuinely angry now, and Melodie's feet begin to grow crooked from the stress again.

"Whatever the case," the man says in a composed voice, "let's return to the question for a moment. Would it be correct to say that you saw your sister was at risk of dying but you chose not to intervene, that's to say you decided not to call the doctor or the emergency services?"

"No, that's not correct. We didn't see that my sister was at risk of passing, we saw that she was very tired and that she wanted to rest and was sinking into a deeper and deeper sleep, and finally she passed, but we didn't know that beforehand."

"Alright," the man says, "let's phrase it another way. You saw that she was slipping away and you didn't find that reason enough to intervene. Is that correct?"

"I did intervene. I did help. I lay down next to her and held her hands the whole time. I took care of her the whole time, the whole time."

"But you didn't think that her 'slipping away' was a reason to seek medical help?"

"No," says Melodie. "No. She didn't need any medical help. She needed love. She needed me. She needed to know I was there. That she was allowed to let go."

"When you say it like that it does sound as though you saw it coming."

"No," says Melodie, "not true. We didn't think she was going to leave us. I didn't know that until she'd truly gone. We didn't know. Yes, looking back on it now, I can see it was a process that would lead to that, but at the time we experienced it step by step."

"Alright. I think we are going round in circles. A little about your housemates. Is it correct that you sensed they thought the same way you did, but you didn't speak about it?"

"We sensed it from each other, yes," Melodie says.

"And you didn't talk about it?"

"No," says Melodie, "we went through it all together in silence."

And with this she is not being entirely accurate in her rendering of the events, whether deliberately or not, we can't judge that, it could be that she has forgotten of course, she often remembers things differently than we do, but we both quite clearly heard Muriel finish her sentence later that evening and ask "Shouldn't we call a doctor? Or an ambulance?" And in response, Melodie said very softly, "Hush now. Let her be. She is so tired. She's ready to let go." After which we heard some shuffling and Muriel's shaky voice whispering "Oh okay, right." This was quite a long time after Elisabeth had lost consciousness, and Petrus didn't say anything, and Muriel was quiet then, and they stayed sitting like that, while Melodie very slowly and quite audibly breathed in and out with her feet clenched together, and soon after this Melodie said that Elisabeth had passed.

Died we'd say, but Melodie preferred not to use that word. Much too direct. And that might well be the problem with this conversation, that Melodie would prefer not to describe things too directly, because the people who are asking the questions seem nice, but they don't understand her very well, and neither does she understand them. The same questions and the same answers repeat and repeat until the dedicated woman says she's heard enough. Melodie is taken back to her cell and immediately goes and sits cross-legged on the bed, which isn't the best position for blood flow to her feet, but it helps her to relax her cramped toes, and relaxation is essential for sensitive people like Melodie, particularly at moments like these when she misses her mother.

20

We are psychological resistance. For years we have been the stick that Petrus was beaten with whenever he didn't want to do something or got angry about something, and now, lying under his thin sheet on the plastic bunk in his cell, in an attempt to catch just a small amount of sleep because he wasn't able to during the night, he whacks himself with it. The sheet goes up and down to the fast rhythm of his breathing, his back and hands are sweaty. His legs want to kick, his arms want to hit, his fists want to tear the sheet in two, his head wants to bang against the wall. Why does he have to stay here if they've finished questioning him? Why have they left him alone for so long without telling him what's going to happen? He wants to scream but he clenches his teeth and remains lying there. I'm suffering from psychological resistance, he says to himself, it's just resistance. And he thinks of the things that Melodie has taught him about us.

"When you feel resistance, it can help to picture it as a big round bale of hay that you are pushing against with all your weight. In the beginning you think your resistance isn't changing but if you keep on pushing you slowly begin to feel the bale giving a little. It all starts to loosen up a bit. And that's the start of relaxation."

Over the past few days he has pushed hundreds of hay bales around in his head, at first leaning on them gently, as Melodie had explained, but later he pushed the bales away from him with both hands. He kicked them away, he knocked them over, he pulled them apart and threw the hay up in the air so it could float on the relaxing gusts of his breath. But now it feels as though we have changed from a bale into a mountain, a mountain resting on top of him and pushing him down, and no matter what he comes up with to try to get rid of us, the pressure on his chest only grows.

"Resistance isn't a thought but a feeling," Melodie had said. "First there is the stimulus, something you perceive. For example, me asking you to share your feelings. Next comes the fear. You're frightened. The thought of having to share your feelings is threatening to you, for whatever reason. Probably something from your early childhood. Your system protests. And then the resistance comes. Your body says no. Your muscles clench. Your jaw clenches. You pull in your belly. And only then, when the feeling of resistance is fully present do the thoughts come. That I'm too interfering, or that Muriel is taking too long to learn her part, or that you want a cigarette, or a beer, or a cheese sandwich. These are all thoughts that turn up to explain the feeling of resistance. But what it's really about is the feeling. The feeling of resistance, and beneath that, the feeling of fear. If you can make contact with that, you'll truly understand where your resistance is coming from. Then you'll be able to heal your wounds. Then you'll be able to open up. Then you will make progress. But you have to let go of the thoughts for a moment to give the feelings a chance."

Petrus has tried, he really has, to let go of his thoughts. But there are too many of them. Too many thoughts about why he is lying here now, without freedom of movement, without daylight, with the only bright spot being the fact that he's allowed to go outside to smoke twice a day. Too many thoughts about guilt. Someone must be to blame that he has been accused of something that absolutely isn't his fault; that he's been unfairly locked up and left all alone. But who? His thoughts bounce back and forth, from Melodie to Muriel to Elisabeth to society to Maruko to the woman in the interview room who had looked at him in total disbelief because he hadn't thought anything, and back to Melodie.

He'd trusted Melodie. They all had. If she didn't know what was good for her sister, how on earth should he have known? If she hadn't seen that Elisabeth needed help, how should he have seen? If she hadn't thought that you should call the doctor if someone is ill, because otherwise the police could take you away, how should he have known? And why is he the one locked up by the police? Why can't he go outside when he wants to? Is he supposed to wait on his own until something happens, while Melodie surely knows that his emotions always turn inwards when he has to spend too long alone. She is the one who told him this, so why hasn't she arranged for his release yet? Why hasn't she taken responsibility herself so that he and Muriel could stay home and wait for everything to be resolved? And you could point a finger at Muriel too. Why was she so quiet that evening? She's always talking, or humming, or singing, or what is supposed to pass for singing, in that infuriating, shaky voice of hers, but when Elisabeth was lying on the bed dying, Muriel only asked Melodie one question and after that she shut up entirely.

"Your housemate lies there dying before you and you think of nothing?" He wonders what Melodie and Muriel would have replied.

And then Elisabeth herself. Pushing against the ever heavier hay bale that symbolizes us, he comes to the conclusion that Elisabeth had always been a millstone around the commune's neck. In all those years he'd barely got to know her and that's because, he thinks, Elisabeth was never a fully-fledged member of the group, but more like someone they'd taken on out of kindness, partly because she was Melodie's sister, partly because she needed a healthy social environment, people she could talk to and who could keep her company, that's why it feels extra painful that the people who arrested him and his housemates are totally blind to the failings of society, which damaged Elisabeth so much, which left her seriously ill, something the group tried to deal with as best it could. The consequence being that they are the scapegoat now, as if it's their fault that after all the things Elisabeth went through she reached a point where she could no longer carry on. As if the commune was the cause of her problems instead of the life buoy that had kept her afloat for years, even though she'd been drowning for so long already. This is how the capitalist neoliberal system lays the blame on the wrong side of the line, Petrus thinks, pummelling the hay bale in his mind with his fists, you could see it in the fact that the detectives only asked questions about their life in the commune and didn't want to know about anything else Elisabeth had experienced, things he doesn't know much about himself, but which Melodie has referred to often enough, which had to do with their family in any case and made her so vulnerable that she finally had no energy left to keep on living. A society that treats the death of a damaged person in this way is sick itself, he thinks, kneeing the hay in his imagination a few more times, but it doesn't help; each time he opens his eyes he finds himself alone in a very small room whose walls seem to be slowly tipping toward him, and he can still feel us weighing down heavily on his chest, however slowly and deeply he breathes, the way he learned to with Maruko, the man from the nine-day process, whom he has always really admired, but now that Petrus is so entrenched in us that he can hardly breathe he remembers that he sometimes felt like he was suffocating during Maruko's guided meditations because Maruko always said that he had to wait until the exhalation collided with the inhalation, which Petrus had never fully understood, so that he kept waiting too long before inhaling, ending up almost hyperventilating every time. And during that period, when they were going through the nine-day process, but also afterwards, when they listened to the sound recordings of it, he'd always thought it was his fault, that he was doing something wrong. But now that Elisabeth is dead he's begun to suspect that Maruko himself wasn't trustworthy. Because Maruko claims that anyone who wants to is capable of living without food, but if you look at how many people have actually managed it, you can see that it's a feat only a rare few dedicated people can pull off, people like Maruko, and maybe Petrus himself in the future, if he keeps on practising, and possibly Melodie too, but certainly not everybody, and so it is highly dangerous to promise everyone that this path can be followed successfully, and the only motivation to do a thing like that that Petrus can think of is greed, because it cost quite a lot of money to go through the nine-day process under Maruko's guidance, they'd had to save up for a long time, and the more people who took part the richer Maruko would become, and he'd noticed these things when they'd first started looking into light nutrition, but he still agreed with Melodie and Muriel that the investment was more than worth it, that all those books and courses might be expensive but they could give you a priceless amount of freedom, while now, now that he's lying all on his own in a much too tiny room with a large invisible suffocating hay bale on top of him, he has to admit that he hasn't gained any freedom but rather lost it, and this thought makes him so angry that he sits up.

"Calm down, Petrus, breathe calmly," he hears Melodie saying in his thoughts. "Let it come. Let the resistance in."

But we are too much, we are too big. Blood rises to his head, his muscles tense, and this is the moment where Melodie would normally say that perhaps he should go outside to cool off and walk the anger out of his body, but he can't, he can't go outside, and because he wants to nevertheless, he stands up and begins to push at the door, using his hands, his shoulders, his back. He pushes and pushes and pushes. He kicks, he batters, he pounds. He screams.

"Let me out! For fuck's sake. Fucking let me out."

He slams his fist against the door, three times, four times, until his hand begins to bleed. And then he cries. And then he lies down on the floor. And then we've gone. Vanished. Petrus surrenders.

"Are you alright?" he hears Melodie say. "Can I take your hand? Good that you're back with us, Petrus. What just happened was very painful. Very painful for all of us. This behaviour of yours wouldn't be accepted by everyone. This aggression. We all feel it very deeply when you scream and stamp. But we love you, Petrus. Unconditionally. We believe in you. You are not your resistance. I believe in you. I believe in your potential. You're not there yet but we are going to get there together."

And it is clear again in his mind why he went to live with Melodie—because she is the only person who can handle it when he is tormented by us. The only person who accepts him, with or without us. The only person who wants him, despite his bad behaviour. Petrus brings his damaged hand to his mouth. He sucks his knuckles. The taste of his own blood reassures him. Maybe he should lie back down on his bed. But along with us, all of the energy has gone too, so he remains lying on the floor and his eyes close and there is Melodie again, Melodie standing next to a strongman game with a megaphone shouting "We are love, we are love," and he hits her head with a big hammer that falls from her trunk and bounces away, as big waves of orange juice gush out of her neck, and he has to jump very high in the air to avoid the stream of orange juice coming at him, as high as a Ferris wheel; and floating in the sky above the fairground he wonders whether he'll crash down into the haystack now but Melodie's head tells him he won't because he must remember that they are together, they are the only ones who are truly together, because they dare to really connect with each other, and together is stronger than alone, isn't it, Petrus, she says, give me your heart for a moment, and he is about to reach for his heart but her head is much too big and her voice much too loud, she screams and shouts like a drunk, and at that sound Petrus wakes up, all stiff from lying on the floor; he has no idea what time it is, but it seems a screaming prisoner has just been brought in, and soon someone will come to his cell with food, and who knows, he might be able to smoke another cigarette, one more, he'll quit once he's back home again, only not right now, now he needs them, all alone with his inward-turning energy; but Melodie will understand, there are so many things she has already understood and forgiven, and he resolves to remind himself of them next time he feels us rising up at something Melodie has said or done. After all, we are just a feeling, and only by feeling us and letting go of his thoughts about what everyone else is doing wrong will he be able to conquer us.

21

We are the preliminary findings. Printed in tripli-
cate and stapled together. We are on a grey tabletop
with a modular ceiling above it, which is covered in
tiny holes, while Liesbeth, Asif, and Ton are having
a meeting about us. Ton is speaking and as he
speaks he covers us in his saliva in which tiny frag-
ments of the egg sandwich he had for breakfast can
be detected, while Asif, somewhat absentmindedly,
strokes us with his fingertips and Liesbeth's full
focus is on the top right-hand corner of the first
page of her copy. She makes a very small dog-ear and
uses the top of her nail to rub the fold tighter. Then
she unfolds the corner again and makes a new tight
fold right next to the first one, and right next to that
another one, and another one, until she has created
a fold that runs exactly along the top right corner of
the block of text, along the last letter of our first
line, the last h of death: *Victim found dead in her home
on 27th July following notification of death.*

"Well," says Ton, who received us an hour ago by
email but hasn't had time to read us yet, and which
he tries to do inconspicuously as he talks, "quite an
unusual bunch of people this lot. Of course, it isn't
our job to judge. People are allowed to make unusual
choices. But if it leads to a person dropping dead ..."

Climb down off your pulpit and get to the point is what we say. No need to repeat us like water-cooler chat; Liesbeth has written us down clearly enough. But apparently some people can't resist the temptation to talk about what has already been written down clearly.

"But anyway," Ton says, hitting our front with his flat palm, "the matter at hand. What are the facts we have here?" His eyes glide over our summary. "Malnutrition: established; deteriorating health, two timeframes. Yes, good that you have looked at two different periods. Suspects no longer remember. Did not notice failing health. Hmm." He clicks his tongue. "That's a real pity, isn't it, folks?"

"What's a pity?" Liesbeth asks as she runs her nail back and forth over the last fold she made.

"Well. All the work the two of you have put into this."

Liesbeth unfolds the dog-ear again. "And what would be a pity about that?"

"Not to knock your work, of course. Oh no. You've done a thorough job. I couldn't have done better myself."

"But?"

"But, well, all in all you haven't been able to find much evidence that we are dealing with criminal offenses. However distressing it is. You'd have to be a very determined public prosecutor to see a case in this."

Asif clears his throat. "Which doesn't mean to say that there is no value in us having recorded all the facts so comprehensively." He coughs. "Liesbeth mainly, of course. I only helped questioning the suspects. And I was very impressed by her thoroughness. It was very educational, Liesbeth. I wanted to tell you that."

"Yes, our Liz is a real little terrier, isn't she?"

"And whatever else, I think we did get the suspects thinking. I genuinely saw some pennies drop during our talks. And even though that isn't strictly part of our remit, it's still—"

"That's nice, Asif, but we're not social workers. We're investigators. We're truth-seekers. And when I see how much work you, particularly Liesbeth then, have put into this case, it just makes me think what a pity. What a pity you've done all that work and yet so few hard facts that you could build a case upon have come to light."

"Mhm, mhm," says Liesbeth, who is now very slowly trying to tear off the corner of the top sheet along the deeply ingrained fold.

"And also because I said from the start that this would be a difficult case. To prove any accountability, I mean. If in the end it has to come down to the question of whether these people should have thought of seeking medical help. For which you are also dependent on the witness statements. That's a lot of hard nuts to crack."

"If the judicial authorities decide to pursue this, they can consult expert witnesses," Liesbeth says. The corner is almost free now.

Ton leans back and folds his hands behind the crook of his head. "And then they'd have to claim those people should have realized that their housemate was in a poor state? What kind of experts would they be? Doctors? Psychologists?"

Liesbeth rolls the torn-off paper triangle between her fingers. "We have proof that malnutrition was the cause of death. And we have proof that the suspects spent all their time with the victim, up to the moment she died," she says in a measured tone. "So it's up to the judiciary to decide whether the suspects should have realized that the victim was malnourished, and whether they should have taken action; I would say myself that the connection between nutrition and survival may be assumed to be well-known."

"At the same time, they are very vulnerable people," Asif says.

"Vulnerable, yes," Ton nods. "Bonkers, in fact."

"No," Asif says, "Not mad. Vulnerable. I know you all think that this is nonsense but it isn't. These people have one or multiple psychiatric disorders which have affected their ability to function in our society. And perhaps it would be better if these people got more help. But we don't live in a world like that at all. So the least we can do is to take their impairments seriously."

Ton raises his hands. "Sorry, Asif. I didn't know you'd get angry. I was only joking. It's alright to keep things a little lighthearted at times, right? What do you think, Liz?"

"Whatever, Ton," Liesbeth replies.

"Alright then, where were we? Recommendation to the public prosecutor's office. I'd be a little cautious myself. There are a lot of overambitious young ladies there these days. This case is a sign of that too. I mean, you might wonder whether we should have started up this whole investigation. Because I'd wager that nothing else will happen. This will end up on a pile for eighteen months until one of those donkey-work jurists glances at it and it is dismissed—too complicated, too little chance of success, minimal societal gain. Slap, one case less on the list. Long live efficiency." And he pushes us away with a nonchalant gesture.

Asif drums the tabletop with his fingers.

"Or do I sound too cynical?" Ton asks. "I'm an old hand on the job, of course. I mean, these are wonderful findings. Beautifully phrased. Well supported. But there's not much hope it will be pursued. All that work. Sorry for saying so. You really did well. But all that work. For nothing in the end, right? For nothing. All your good work. And in retrospect the prosecutor could have told you that beforehand."

"Yes," says Liesbeth, inhaling deeply through her nose. "Thank you, Ton, for this staggering analysis of our investigation. Very nice. I'll give the prosecutor a quick call. Release them?"

"Release them. That woman is driving the detention guards crazy. She keeps asking for organic vegetables. Give them a few screaming junky thieves, much more convivial. We're a police station not a nuthouse." He rubs his forehead. "Boy oh boy oh boy. What a case. Bunch of anorexics."

"Okay, Ton," says Liesbeth. She pushes back her chair and grabs her copy of the text from the table. Her half-full coffee mug tips over and its contents spill on the table, onto Asif's trousers, and Liesbeth leaves the room.

"Hey," says Ton. "Liesbeth?"

Asif shakes his head. "Nice one, Ton."

"Me? I didn't spill coffee over your trousers."

"You could be a bit more tactful though. It's hard enough for her with her daughter. Why do you think this case is so important to her?"

"Her daughter? What's the matter with her?"

Asif gets up and wipes his trousers. "Unbelievable this. How long have you and 'Liz' been working together? Go and ask her what the matter with her daughter is. That's what colleagues do. Can you clean up the rest?"

And as Asif walks away and Ton stays behind on his own, we'd like to speak for ourselves for a moment.

Victim found dead in her home on 27th July following notification of death to the out-of-hours GP service. After examining the body, the duty doctor reported the case to the local coroner because a natural death could not be ascertained. The latter informed the local CID who attended the site and arrested the victim's three housemates upon suspicion of culpable homicide, according to article 307 of the penal code.

Forensic anatomical research of the body indicated that the victim died of malnutrition. The investigating team focused on the question of whether the three suspects, who were present at the death and had also lived with the victim in the period preceding her death, could be held responsible due to neglecting to signal her deteriorating state or call in the necessary medical assistance. Given this, two timeframes preceding the death have been investigated.

First of all the period of several weeks before the victim's death, in which her health must have visibly deteriorated.

It was ascertained that suspects could have observed various signs that indicated deteriorating health, but they didn't recognize these signs as such. Signs which were said to have been observed were not brought into connection with malnutrition at the time, according to the suspects. Amongst those mentioned were increasing tiredness and decreasing talkativeness. Suspect Melodie van H., also sister of the victim, explained that she thought this was caused by a busier and more demanding schedule due to daily visits to their senile mother's nursing home, and also the accompanying emotional burden. Suspect Petrus Z. stated that he hadn't thought about it. Suspect Muriel de V. stated that she no longer remembered clearly. All three suspects stated that their housemate had always been "weak" and "needed help and support" [quote Melodie van H.], whereby the signs of physical degeneration may not have been noticed.

Second timeframe the investigation focused upon was the evening of the death. It was ascertained that the deceased had let it be known that she was "very tired" and "could no longer go on." Suspects stated that they did not think of seeking medical assistance. They gave different reasons for this. Melodie van H. stated that it was a process she wanted to make space for, during which she did not think of the probable outcome of her sister dying. She also stated that her sister was ready for the next step and that she does not perceive death as a negative event. Petrus Z. stated that he was trying to be present in the moment and that he didn't think of intervening. Muriel de V. stated that she can no longer remember.

The three suspects do not seem to pose any danger to society and can be released.

When deciding whether or not to press charges, one might consider the question of whether the suspects can be *held accountable for failing to seek medical assistance, given that awareness of the need for this could reasonably have been expected of them. The psychological vulnerability of the suspects should also be examined in this respect.*

22

We are a pen, a brand-new white pen with the police department's logo on the side. We have been lying on a pile of unlined A4 paper on the table in a worried woman's cell since yesterday morning, waiting for her to do something with us. Before we got here, we spent months in a large crate, along with hundreds of other identical pens, until we were taken out and moved to a pen pot that contained some pencils and a few older, more experienced pens, and now it looks like we'll finally be able to do what we have been preparing for all our short life. Writing. Being held by someone between thumb, index, and middle finger, placed against a piece of paper and then making words together with the writer, maybe even sentences, even though that's not so common anymore according to the older pens, people prefer to use their computers or telephones, which the older pens find an eternal shame, a loss for humankind and for penkind too, since the pen is the most direct medium to connect human to text, they say, the only medium in which the contents are contained not just in the words but also in the way they are written, that is to say the exact way the writer has allowed the pen to glide over the paper, hurried or slow, hesitant or self-assured, careless or precise, so that it is a genuine loss that today the pen has largely been condemned to the writing of shopping and to-do lists, while the really important texts, like letters and even scribbled notes are farmed out to those standoffish devices.

Scribbled notes. As a newcomer we don't really have an opinion yet, about those devices, but *scribbled* is a nice word. We hope we'll be scribbling a note. Or a letter, because a letter is very long, they told us, and once it's finished it goes somewhere, and so we go too, a little bit, in any case the ink that has come out of us, and then someone else spends time reading it. A letter or a note would be our preference, one of the two.

It would be our first time, if it does happen—the woman looks even more nervous than we are. She has picked us up a few times; one time she brought our tip really close to the paper but she put us down again and went back to her bed where she sat cross-legged with her eyes shut. She's sitting there now like that, leaning against the cell wall with her eyes closed, rubbing her belly with her hands. We can hear her breathing deeply and then she opens her eyes wide and says, "Okay, okay Muriel."

She lets herself slide from the bed and crawls to the little table we are on. It's too low and too small to be used for serious writing, so it won't be a letter, if it's anything at all. Again we are picked up, she clenches us with her sweaty fingers, the side of her middle finger from below, thumb and index fingers from the sides. Then the miracle happens. Our tip touches the paper and we begin carefully to glide, leaving behind a trace of dark-blue ballpoint ink on the white surface. We make words in neat joined-up letters.

Dear Mum and Dad,

I am writing you

A letter! Yes! A letter! To her parents, at that. Our very first time and already being used for a letter.

But our joy is premature. The sentence stops. She shoves the sheet with the first words under the pile and begins again, now in a different handwriting, larger and rounder, with letters that are not connected.

Things that nourish me

She draws a line under the words *Things that nourish me*. A recipe then? Or a shopping list?

Things that nourish me

1. *Taking myself seriously*
2. *Feeling my feelings*
3. *Not being dependent on my parents*
4. *Singing with others*

This is still all quite new to us, writing lists, but we don't think the things she has written down are edible. Nor can you buy them in a shop. Maybe it's a kind of to-do list after all.

5. *Reflecting on what is good (for myself and the world)*
6. *Giving and receiving love*
7. *Being open about my emotions*
8. *Spreading my wings and flying away*

She takes a deep breath. "Yes," she says out loud, "I matter. I make my own choices. I am light." She closes her eyes and breaths in and out three times. "I am light."

She wipes her hands on her trousers, which is rather necessary, her fingers are so slippery that we almost keep sliding out.

Things that do not nourish me

Why would she write them down, the things that don't nourish her? She can just simply not buy them, or not do them, right? She doesn't need a list for this, does she?

1. *Repetitive negative thoughts*
2. *Thinking that I am hungry*
3. *Guilt*
4. *Chocolate eclairs*
5. *Raspberry tart with cream and transparent jelly*
6. *Herring with onion*
7. *Thoughts about food*
8. *Calculating calorie intake and consumption in my head*
9. *Keeping myself awake with thoughts about food*

10. *Bread with chocolate sprinkles and cheese*
11. *Being afraid that I will die if I don't eat enough*
12. *Fear*

Strange, there are things you can buy in a shop on the list, but she isn't planning to. And clearly she knows this is a bit odd, a reverse shopping list, because now she has crossed it out with fierce strokes. Which is a new experience for us—crossing out—making wordless thick lines, back and forth and back and forth without detour. And, as though she is shocked by the crossing out, as though she wants to make amends, she draws a few shaky hearts and flowers next to the list of things that feed her. Then she puts the piece of paper with the two lists on the floor and continues on a new sheet.

Nourishing affirmations

1. *I am light*
2. *I sing from my heart*
3. *I spread my wings and fly away*
4. *Everything I need is already here*
5. *Everything that I need is already there*
6. *I have everything I need*

She picks up the sheet with the nourishing affirmations, whatever they are, and sits on her bed. She begins to read the lines aloud, but her voice betrays the fact she might burst into tears at any moment, and when she gets to *I sing from my heart* the tears begin to flow.

Emotions can come out when a person starts to write, we were prepared for that, but this is still a surprise, that those lines upset her so much, given they sound quite positive. Maybe they have a deeper meaning. Maybe this is a poem, you hear that too, that people write poems that don't rhyme. Or it's a kind of sad song, only without music.

"Everything I need is already here," she says, snivelling. "Everything I need is already here. I have everything I need."

Repeating the sentences makes her cry even harder. She shakes and jerks like a small child and we even think we hear her say "Mummy," which isn't such a strange thought because as soon as she's calmed down a bit, she crawls back to the table and takes the bottom sheet—the letter, yes, that was the letter—from the pile.

Dear Mum and Dad,

I am writing you

And she writes in the same flowing slow handwriting as at the start, pausing at times, with our tip still to the paper, and then quickly writing on. Not much longer and then our first letter is a fact.

this letter in police custody. My housemates and I have been arrested upon suspicion of culpable homicide because Elisabeth died. The police said it was from malnutrition. I know that the last time I came round we argued because I was so thin. And I think it was best for you and for me that we didn't see each other anymore after that. Because I really did believe that this was the right path for me and it wasn't nice that you wouldn't support me in it, not for me and neither for you. I don't know how this all could have happened. The police said that we could have seen earlier that Elisabeth wasn't doing well. And I had already worked out that we would probably run out of energy when we started visiting Melodie and Elisabeth's mother every day. She was moved to a care home a while ago and we wanted to spend as much time with her as possible because they weren't taking good enough care of her there. But this was probably a bit too much for Elisabeth. Looking back I think that she and I weren't entirely ready to give up food. And I think that you might have seen that the last time I visited you. And now it's very sad that Elisabeth has died. In a certain way it might be the best thing for her because she always seemed very unhappy. But I do ask myself whether we could have prevented it. The evening that she died I did think of calling an ambulance but I didn't dare say anything and then after that it was too late. And there was something beautiful about it too. The way she died was very peaceful, it really was. But then the doctor came, one we didn't know because our own GP wasn't on call, and he thought it was all very irregular and then the police came and so now I'm here. And I've started to have doubts about everything myself. And now I don't know exactly why I'm writing this letter but

She stops for a moment and then, out of the blue, she puts the end of us in her mouth and begins to slowly turn her tongue around us. So this is what they meant by other things, that you aren't only used for writing but that they also do other things with you. Clicking, twiddling, biting, sucking. It feels a little strange, but certainly not unpleasant.

in any case I'd like to apologize to you because I think you will be disappointed in me because of everything that has happened. It's also a shame that we no longer see each other because of this. But I wanted to say that none of it was deliberate! And if you'd like maybe we could meet up some time to talk. I've come to some realizations about the past and I think it would be good to share them with you.

Best wishes

She holds back for a moment and squeezes our tip. Her fingers have again become really sweaty.

and a hug from your daughter Muriel

And the woman, your daughter Muriel, doesn't take this paper back to her bed but leaves it lying on the table along with us as she stretches out on the bed, probably to have a rest after the writing. She begins to hum softly, hesitantly at first but after a while a melody begins to take shape and once it is there, the words come too.

As I were a walking down by the seaside
I saw a red herring washed up by the tide,
And that little herring I took home and dried.
Don't you think I done well with my jolly herring.

And she lies there a while, singing away with her hands tapping the beat on her stomach, and even though it doesn't sound entirely good, she seems to be enjoying it, but then suddenly there's a loud noise behind her cell door and the singing stalls in her throat. She shoots to her feet, grabs the letter and all the other bits of paper, and shoves them under her pillow. She looks around her cell as though she suspects someone is looking at her. Then she gets the letter out from under her pillow again and puts it on the floor. She takes us from the table and begins to cross out all the lovely words we made together. She covers the line about doing the calculations in a thick dark-blue stripe, and the two sentences where she's wondering whether they could have prevented it because she had thought of calling an ambulance, and the line where she writes that she's started to doubt everything. And a few more sentences that come after the crossed-out lines. She sighs deeply a few times, folds the letter, and again, and again, and slides it into her left trouser pocket. A new, empty sheet is now at the top of the pile, and clenching the end of us between her teeth she looks at the blank paper and we start to ask ourselves whether the shock may have given her writer's block but then she takes us out of her mouth and begins to write.

Dear housemates,

*I would like to tell you something. Over the past
days I have started to have serious doubts*

Another letter. Our first time with Muriel and already
two letters, two mysterious shopping lists, mouth
contact, and a poem that made her cry. When we tell
this to the others they won't want to believe it.

She rolls us a few times between her teeth. Then
she crosses out *started to have serious doubts.*

been thinking a lot.

She changes the full stop after *a lot* into a comma.

, and reflecting.

And crosses out this last full stop too.

on the way we live.

She pauses for a moment. Then she crosses out the
full stop again and adds the word *together.* And then
she draws an upside-down roof between *we* and *live
together* and adds the words *want to* before crossing
out *on the way we want to live together* entirely.

on the way I want to live.

"Yes," she says, "the way I want to live."

*I was very shocked when the police told me that
Elisabeth had died of malnutrition. But to be
honest I think I had seen it coming to some extent.*

This letter seems even more difficult to write than the previous one. She writes slowly and doesn't press hard and stops each time to change things. Now she does it again. She takes a deep breath and leans back. Then she shakes her head and crosses out all of the last sentence.

*I hadn't seen it coming at all. But in retrospect I
don't think it's that surprising. Our idea of living
off light was very inspiring to me. I liked the idea
of no longer being dependent on anything.*

Again she leans back, and *no longer being dependent on anything* gets crossed out.

going through that process together.

She gets to her feet. "I am enough," she says out loud as she turns us around between her fingers. "I am enough. I am enough. I am enough." And then she sits down again.

*But to be honest I'm afraid that it's not possible.
You see I was hungry almost all the time and it
often stopped me from sleeping. And I think
Elisabeth might have had the same thing. And I
don't want to blame you*

She crosses out *you* and changes it into *us*.

us for anything, but I think that we

"No," she says. And the last sentence vanishes under a thick layer of ink.

So in retrospect I wonder whether our way of life was right for Elisabeth. Because maybe she wasn't really ready for it. Or the issue I have, that the thought you need food really gets in the way. And that's why I've also started to wonder whether I really fit in the group. Because my impression is that the two of you can handle it a bit better. I have tried to learn from you but failed each time. And now that Elisabeth is dead I don't think I'm ready to die too. I'm really frightened of that now. And maybe it would teach me a lot but I'm still afraid that I can't do it.

"No," she says, squeezing and almost crushing us. "No. I really can't do that."

And that's why I think it would be better if I moved out. I'm really very sorry and I will miss you because I've learned so much from you both. I hope you will understand and that we can remain friends. I wish you all the best.

Love, Muriel

She sighs again. "I am enough, I am enough, I am enough," she says. Then she clutches us between her teeth again, folds the letter a few times, and puts it in her right trouser pocket. And why she needs to do this we don't know but she begins to tear the remaining blank sheets of paper, first in half, then in half again, and then again, until there is a small pile of little white squares on her table. She sweeps up all the squares in her hands, throws them up in the air, and allows them to fall on her head and her shoulders, her legs crossed in a lotus position, and she stays like this, covered in small white shreds of paper, with us in her mouth and a folded letter in each trouser pocket, until someone comes to tell her that she's free to go home.

23

We are cognitive dissonance. We are the unpleasant sensation you get when reality turns out not to match your beliefs; when, based on your own behaviour, you find yourself to be more narrow-minded, petty, and oversensitive than you ever thought. We are the grimace that crosses your face for those few seconds until you've been able to come up with a story in which the facts, or your own relationship to them, have been twisted so that everything tallies again. We are the mother and father of your self-deception.

You don't need to be ashamed of us, you're not the only one. Just look at Melodie. Over the past days and nights her brain has had to work overtime to make all the facts and questions about how she acted during her sister's death chime with the image she has of herself. Armed with enough stories to not only convince herself but also her housemates that none of the three of them can be held responsible, she follows the guard through the long corridor of the detention centre. At the desk she is given the things she had handed in at the beginning: her ID card, her purse, telephone, the keys to her house. To our house, she corrects herself, it's our house, and she follows the guard along more corridors and down the stairs to the waiting room on the ground floor where Muriel and Petrus are waiting for her.

"At last," she says. She goes over to Muriel, wraps her arms around her, and presses herself to her. "What a nightmare."

She feels Muriel stiffen at the embrace. She's seriously lost the connection, she thinks to herself, and lets go of Muriel to hug Petrus, receiving the same response, and also making out the smell of cigarettes.

"At last. Thank god. How hellish this has been? Hellish. What happened to your hand?"

"Nothing," says Petrus. He looks at his hand. "Banged it."

"Phew. I was worried it was all too much for you without us." Melodie looks over her shoulder at the guard. "Can we go now?" she asks.

"You can go, yes. Have a nice day now." The man turns and walks away.

"Unbelievable, the way we've been treated. As though we were criminals. Are you coming?"

Muriel and Petrus stand up. They walk through the revolving door one after another and then stop, blinking at the bright sunlight outside.

"Ah. Light. At last. This feels like a homecoming. This is already a homecoming, don't you think? The air, the light, you, us. How wonderful. Don't you think?"

"Yes," says Muriel. "Lovely, yes."

They begin to walk.

"How hellish this has been, how hellish. The way they put us under pressure, over Elisabeth's dead body. The lies. The manipulation. I'm at a loss for words. I simply don't know what to say." Shaking her head, Melodie walks between the other two. "But luckily we're stronger. That's the most important thing, that we are strong together. Together we are so strong! Even when we are not together. Every time I was at the end of my tether I felt the two of you, I felt your support. That's what we have built together, isn't it?" She looks from Petrus to Muriel and back. "We have each other. That makes us extra strong, doesn't it? Didn't you get that feeling too, that we were helping each other, even though we weren't together?"

And now we begin to set in motion the cogs of self-deception within Muriel and Petrus too. Neither of them have had the feeling over the last few days that they were in contact with the others. They felt alone and cut off. But now they realize that that feeling isn't befitting of a resident of the Sound & Love Commune, and they quickly begin to edit their memories of their experiences in the cells.

"Yes, I felt that too," says Muriel as she pictures the moments when she tried to sing and meditate to comfort herself. "Not as strongly as you, I don't think, but when I meditated or did the affirmations, I did feel something like that."

"I thought about you two a lot, yes," says Petrus truthfully. He wipes the sweat from his forehead.

Melodie nods, her eyebrows lifted high. "Yes, yes. Of course there were difficult moments too. You weren't always at the top of my mind. But as soon as I got back in contact with myself, I immediately felt your presence. Very special. Fantastic that you meditated, Muriel, under the circumstances. Well done."

They turn the corner and walk along the pavement next to a busy cycle path, heading toward the railway underpass.

"And the food. All of it treated with pesticides and processed. I just didn't eat anything, I only drank some water. I think it would have made me ill. What a trauma, all of this, what a horrible trauma. After everything I did for her, we did for her."

The other two remain silent.

"So painful the way they twisted our story. So painful. They acted like we'd stopped eating entirely. As though we'd let Elisabeth starve to death."

At the entrance to the underpass the pavement becomes too narrow for the three of them. Melodie speeds up and goes ahead of Muriel and Petrus. Half turning, she says, "It was almost impossible to explain. At the start, they thought the whole time that we'd stopped eating completely. And that one of us decided how much we ate and when. I really had to expend a lot of energy explaining that properly. That we all decided ourselves what our own limits were."

They come out of the underpass, returning to the bright sunlight. Her arms spread wide, Melodie stops for a moment. "What a pleasure this is. How I missed this." She sets off again, walking backwards now, her face to her two housemates. "I can feel myself filling up with energy, can't you?"

Muriel and Petrus nod. They walk slowly, slightly bent over, like two elderly people shuffling to the supermarket for their daily shop.

"How exhausting this has been," says Melodie. "Aren't you tired? Would you share? Petrus, I see that your fists are clenched. Do you think you can manage to relax them again? We're safe now. Relax and let go. The rest will follow automatically."

They cross the bike path to the traffic lights.

"I'm so grateful that we're together again," Melodie says. "So grateful. Aren't you? Simply to be walking here, simply walking in the sun together."

They are walking in the sun, that is absolutely true. But the other things they are experiencing don't match what they are saying. They say that they are happy to see each other, they say they have missed each other, but beneath that, we are fermenting away. Muriel is beginning to wonder whether she still wants to leave, especially after what Melodie just said about food. She'd forgotten that somewhat, that they were all allowed their own limits. She probably projected her own judgements about herself too much on others, thinking they would judge her if she gave into her feelings of hunger, while that wasn't the case. And now she's walking along with Melodie and Petrus like this, she can no longer imagine throwing everything away that they have together, just because she's hungry. It suddenly seems very unreal that she might say "I'm leaving." After everything they've been through together. And the things they are about to go through, because in the meantime, Elisabeth is still dead, in one way or another she keeps forgetting that, not the fact itself but the practical aspects of it, that they need to arrange a funeral with flowers and a coffin, or a reed basket, mourning cards and a car, Petrus and Melodie can't do that alone, and she wouldn't want that either, they have to do this together. They lost her together and now they have to bury her together, it's obvious. This is their life. Our life, Muriel thinks. My life. I can't just walk away from my own life, can I?

But with the farewell letter in her pocket, she will have to come up with a very good reason as to why she thought very differently about this a few hours ago.

"You look tired," says Melodie. "Closed. You are both really quite closed. Which isn't that odd, given the way they tried to manipulate us. With the story that Elisabeth became malnourished because of us, and that we should have helped her. As if we'd ever forbidden her to eat. Crazy right? Crazy. If we hadn't taken her in to live with us, she would have died much sooner, with her weak constitution. I'm so happy we didn't go along with that nonsense. That we carried on explaining how things really were. Elisabeth could have always told us if she was hungry. Elisabeth's problem wasn't to do with that."

Yes, yes, thinks Petrus, his balled fists hidden deep in his trouser pockets. That's what I'd say too if I was you, that Elisabeth's problem wasn't to do with that. Because if it was, her being dead would be your fault.

They turn onto the big shopping street. It's busy in town, no space to walk next to each other anymore. They walk in silence in a row for a while, Melodie at the front, then Petrus, and behind him Muriel. Then they turn into a side street where the three of them can walk alongside each other again.

"If I'm honest, I did start to doubt myself at times, you know? There were times I thought we might have done something wrong after all. Or thought something wrong, said something wrong. But then I went back to myself and looked inside my own heart and I knew it was all nonsense. It was all a way of belittling us and insulting us. If Elisabeth had needed anything, we really would have noticed. But she always made it very clear that she didn't want help, except the help we already gave her. And each time the doubts came back, I closed my eyes and felt my wisdom. My conviction returned that it was her own choice, that she was ready for the next step. Letting go of her was the best thing we could have done for her. And this goes beyond all the pressure to keep people alive as long as possible, whatever the cost, even in an artificial way with poisonous medicine, without actual contact. It goes beyond guilt and innocence. It goes beyond everything in fact. But I have to say that it was very hard to stick to my own truth. Very hard."

Muriel and Petrus grunt in agreement. They walk slower and slower, as though wanting to delay their return home. They shuffle along the pavement. The sun falls in large square patches on the street, there is barely any shade. Soon they'll reach their front door, and still the stories they tell themselves are not consistent with reality. Petrus tries to work with the resistance he is feeling at the gush of words coming from Melodie, telling himself that dissolving that resistance is the only way forward for himself. Resistance is a feeling, he tells himself. Resistance is a feeling, resistance is a feeling. And the thought that Melodie is talking rubbish because she's trying to justify the fact she wouldn't let us call an ambulance only comes after that. I'm not the one thinking that, it's my resistance. A large hay-stack that will give way if only I can find a calm way to put my shoulder to it. If I can truly feel my resistance, these thoughts will go away.

"To be honest, I ate some bread at the police station," Muriel says.

"I'd noticed that your energy was a little weaker than usual," says Melodie. "But I do understand. It was a disruptive situation. I can imagine you weren't able to connect with the nourishing energy. It will feel different again after a week, I'm sure."

Muriel nods as the part of her that wants to leave asks itself whether she'll still be living with Melodie in a week's time, perhaps she'll leave after five days, if they are able to arrange the funeral quickly, but the part that wants to stay is wondering what the reasons were to leave again. Because if Melodie is right about wisdom, didn't she abandon her own wisdom when she thought she should call a doctor for Elisabeth? Wasn't that the voice of the outside world speaking inside her, saying that she had to do what the outside world thought, namely to call a doctor because somebody was ill, because what is illness in fact, and do doctors always do the right thing, with all that poisonous medicine they prescribe? And isn't Melodie the person who has always been able to bring her in contact with her own feelings, with her inner butterfly? With the feeling that she is valuable, that she doesn't have to do what others expect of her the whole time? That she can unfold her wings and fly away? Wasn't the idea to call an ambulance a spasm of her old self, that was fed by those people from the police?

"I did worry about you," Melodie says. "You are so sensitive to authority. I thought they might have frightened you or made you feel guilty. I mean, it was hard enough for me, and you had to do it all on your own, without our support."

"Yes," says Muriel, and the part that wanted to walk away is already getting more unsteady, weaker, and the part that is writing a new story about her doubts in the police cell is growing bigger and stronger, and the thought that after a predetermined amount of time she will really leave begins to blow away, like the fluff from the dandelions growing between the paving stones of their street, her street, the street they are walking along now, the street with her house on it, their house.

And as Melodie puts her hand in her pocket to get out the house keys, Petrus is pulling straws from the hay bale in his mind and making letters with them on the pavement. An *F*, a *U*, a *C*, a *K*, an *M*, an *E*.

FUCK MELODIE.

24

We are the slow juicer, the most important piece of kitchen equipment in the Sound & Love Commune and Muriel's mainstay. We've missed her. It's been really hard on us, having to wait for her, unemployed, for such a long time. And then those strange people who came into the house and made sarcastic comments about us, very unpleasant. But it won't be long now because we can hear the wind chimes at the front door tinkling.

"Right." Melodie's voice. "Here we are again. How wonderful."

"I can smell perfume," says Petrus. "Or cleaning products. Something lemony."

"That they could do this, eh. Such an invasion of our privacy. The energy in the air. Totally disrupted. And they didn't even go to the trouble of closing the cupboards."

"Bastards," says Petrus, and we start to wonder whether Muriel has come with them or not, but then we hear him say, "Alright, Muriel?"

She's here, she's home. With a bit of luck she'll walk right into the kitchen and give us a silent kiss on our side, or she'll lay her cheek against us. She does that sometimes when she hasn't seen us for half a day or longer.

"Leave her be a moment then," Melodie says.

For a few minutes all we hear is shuffling, sniffing, and sighing.

"Do you want to share something with us, Muriel?" Melodie asks.

And then, at last, we hear her voice. "It's so awful, it's so awful," she sobs. "Elisabeth's airbed, Elisabeth's blanket."

"Yes," says Melodie, "I hadn't thought of that either, that they'd just leave them lying there."

"Do you want—" says Petrus. "Hang on. I'll get you a tissue."

He goes into the kitchen looking for a piece of kitchen paper. He looks concerned. That's not the Petrus we know.

"It doesn't matter, Muriel. It's fine. Have a cry," says Melodie.

Muriel replies but we can't understand her.

"What did you say, Muriel?" Melodie asks.

"If you can let go of me for a moment." Even at this distance we can hear her panting. "Thanks."

"Here," says Petrus.

"Thank you. Sweet of you." Muriel loudly blows her nose.

"Shall I just put the airbed away then?" Petrus asks. "Or would you rather I left it there?"

"Tidy it up, yes. Elisabeth will stay with us whether we take her bed away or not."

"I was talking to Muriel. Muriel? Should I leave her bed there for a while or would you rather not?"

"Um. Yes. No, take it away."

"Yes," says Melodie, "I think that's for the best too."

Silence for a few minutes. It's quite sad about Elisabeth, of course. Logical that Muriel needs a bit of time. But we can't imagine she's not longing for us terribly, that her thoughts as she cries aren't also going out to the matter of what she's going to make shortly. There's still celery in the fridge, highly suitable for a tasty juice with a bit of bite. And in the fruit bowl there's an apple, a bit wrinkled but big enough to add some subtle sweetness. Though two apples would be better. Yet for that they'd have to go shopping first. But if they were going out anyway, they'd also be able to buy carrots, and oranges for fresh orange juice. Orange juice would surely be comforting, though it's always nerve-wracking how Petrus will react to the smell. But that aside, anything is possible. There's a reason we're the Rolls Royce of slow juicers, with the most powerful motor, and two worm wheels rather than one so that our output is thirty percent more than that of more inferior brands and models, and an ingenious output tube to separate the juice from the pulp, so that all the fresh vegetables, nuts, and fruit have been turned into a delicious pure juice within a matter of seconds, as the dry pulp is carried away, and all the vitamins and minerals are preserved, and without the usual noise of other juicers and centrifugal machines.

"This is not a bad thing, Muriel," we hear Melodie say. "I think this is actually very good. Good for you to show your emotions. It's quite a thing to suddenly have to let go."

"Yes," says Muriel. "Yes, sorry. It's also because I'm a bit hungry, I think. Perhaps I could make some vegetable juice for us? I think we still have some celery. And an apple. Or we could go to the shop and buy some carrots and oranges?"

Muriel, a woman after our heart.

"It's okay, Muriel. The emotions are all a bit stronger if you don't distract yourself with food. That's all good. I haven't eaten myself since they took us away, so you can figure out for yourself how I'm doing."

"Yes, you must be hungry too. I'll just check in the kitchen whether—"

"That's very sweet of you but it's not what I meant. I actually meant that I'm very closely attuned to my feelings as far as I'm concerned. And I don't feel the need to anaesthetise them with food. It's better for us to make real contact. Sit together calmly for a while. See whether we can repair the energy a bit. Would you go and make tea instead? And I'll clear a space for our cushions. And some incense sounds like a good idea too, to cleanse the air."

And then the moment finally arrives. Muriel comes into the kitchen. Her face is red and blotchy, there are tears in her eyes, but still the beginnings of a smile appear around her mouth when she sees us. She doesn't kiss us and she doesn't rest her cheek against us, but as she passes she runs her fingertips over our surface as a sign that she's happy to see us. Then she picks up the kettle to make tea.

We've seen Muriel go through this ritual so often we could map out every detail. The way she fills the kettle with water. The glass containers of herbal tea that she gets from the shelf. Compiles a mixture of herbs: camomile, lavender, aniseed. Muriel knows her taste combinations. She drops the herbs into the big thermos flask and waits, rubbing her belly. As soon as the water begins to boil, she moves her hand to the kettle's handle so she can pick it up and pour water into the thermos the very moment the kettle clicks off. She puts the kettle back, waits a while, then turns the top of the flask and waits for a few more moments. Then she pours the yellow liquid into three glasses, which she places on a wooden tray and carries into the living room.

"Thank you, Muriel, that's lovely," we hear Melodie say. "Lovely to be home again. I can feel the energy settling already, can't you?" A moment's silence. "Hm, lavender. Lovely. That's very cleansing too."

"Yes," says Muriel.

"Well, we've got a lot to tell each other, of course, but let's wait a while with that. It causes so much disturbance. Right?"

"Sure," says Petrus.

"By the way, I have a strong feeling that she's still here," Melodie says. "They may have taken her body but she is still here. I can feel her very clearly. And I can feel that everything is good, that she's happy we are back."

The other two say nothing.

"Yes, good not to say anything. Just *be* completely with what there is. That's very good."

Time passes, we find it hard to estimate how much. Ten minutes, twenty, half an hour. Enough time to have produced a healthy amount of hunger-quenching fresh juice even at our impressively low rotational speed of eighty-two revolutions per minute.

"Aren't you having any tea yourself? It will get cold."

"Yes. Sorry. The shops will be shutting soon, I think. So if we still want to buy anything we'll have to leave in a minute."

"You said we still had some celery, didn't you? And an apple?" Melodie says. "We can make something with that, can't we? For whoever wants some later. I think it would be good to take things slowly. Leave some space. Don't jump straight into action mode. Petrus. Won't you have some tea? It's good for you too."

"Won't you have some tea? It's good for you too," we hear him repeat after Melodie. "As if you always know what's good. May I decide that myself? Whether tea is good for me? Elisabeth always had to do what you said the whole time too. And look what happened to her."

Muriel begins to cough.

"I am transparent," says Melodie. "I am transparent, Petrus. Transparent to your anger. It doesn't touch me."

"I'm not angry," says Petrus. "But I'd like to decide myself whether I drink my tea or not."

"Petrus. I get that you are experiencing resistance after everything we have been through. But you yourself once chose to come and live here. You gave yourself that gift because you wanted connection. So if you choose now to break that connection, that's allowed, but then you are choosing in opposition to yourself, against a deep longing of yours to break free of your resistance. I get that you are upset after all the setbacks and the terrible things the police said to us, but then it might be good in any case to recognize those feelings for what they are. So that your reactions are not led by your resistance but by your wisdom. Don't you think?" She pauses for a moment. "Oh look, now Muriel is all upset again. Do you want a tissue?"

"No," sobs Muriel, "I still have the one Petrus gave me. And I'm okay."

"How about you go for a quick walk, Petrus," Melodie says. "Breath of fresh air, until you come to. We'll see you in a bit. Then we'll see you again, rather than your anger."

"Oh yes," says Muriel. "So perhaps you can get some shopping at the same time. I was thinking of carrots and oranges in any case. And the camomile is almost finished. Oh."

The door from the living room into the hall is slammed shut with a bang.

"Petrus?"

"Leave him be a while. We're all tired. I hope he'll calm down a bit." Melodie sighs noisily. "I was already a little concerned the detectives would put funny ideas into his head. I found them really manipulative. Very leading. You really have to be very sure of yourself to carry on believing in our reality. You're a little further in that than he is."

"Yes," says Muriel, and a silence falls that is long enough to make a new suggestion, to make some vegetable juice, for example.

"I'm incredibly happy with you, Muriel," says Melodie. "And I can feel that Elisabeth is too. She's happy that we have all been left together in this, that I don't have to do it alone. Elisabeth's funeral. Petrus's attacks. It's nice to be able to support each other, don't you think?"

"Hm, hm," says Muriel weakly.

"Have a bit more tea."

Muriel doesn't want tea. She wants carrots. She wants oranges. She wants us. And we want her. But Melodie wants her to drink tea first, and then Petrus comes home and they have to meditate together, and after the meditation they have to sing, that they are light and love and sound everywhere, until long after dinnertime. It begins to grow dark outside as the singing finally comes to an end and Muriel is finally able to break free from the others, announcing that she'd like to make some vegetable juice for tomorrow morning. As she opens the fridge and takes out the celery sticks, Melodie comes into the kitchen.

"Should we still use those? They've been in the fridge for a really long time. I don't know whether there's much energy left in them. I'm afraid most of it will have seeped out."

We see Muriel's face contort in the shadows and her hand closes tightly around the celery. You're not going to deprive us of that juice, Melodie, we think, and we know Muriel is thinking the same.

"Or have this apple," Melodie says. "It looks alright still."

Muriel lets her shoulders drop.

"It's hard for you, isn't it?" says Melodie. "I can see that you're having a tough time. Your system has taken a blow. The things you ate there will have contributed. A little bit of juice might be good if you think it will help. Help cut back again."

"Yes," says Muriel in a small voice, "I think it will help."

It's a start. It's a start, Muriel. No carrots and oranges but better than nothing.

As Melodie returns to the living room, Muriel begins to peel the apple and cut it into chunks. She plugs us in and then at last, at last our patented double worm wheel can turn again. Tears slide down her cheeks as she shovels the dry apple pulp into her mouth with a small spoon. She pours the juice into three tiny glasses, puts them on a wooden chopping board, wipes the tears from her cheeks, and leaves the kitchen holding it.

25

We are light. In an undulating orange shaft we fall on the fleece blankets of the three inhabitants of the Sound & Love Commune who are lying on their airbeds in the living room. Melodie, asleep with a frown on her forehead and her front teeth over her sucked-in bottom lip. Petrus, totally relaxed, his mouth half-open, a touch of saliva twinkling in the right-hand corner, completely surrendered to sleep. And Muriel, wide-awake as so often at this time. Most of her face is in shadow but her wide eyes shine. We've known those eyes for so long. We can remember how blue they were when she was born. The way she was unaccustomed to us at first. Unaccustomed yet curious. Hungry for sensations. But now it seems like her eyes don't want us anymore, as though they'd rather not see us anymore.

We aren't the type of phenomenon that easily doubts itself, but now Muriel has begun to cry, we wonder whether it's our fault, whether she's disappointed in us because she genuinely thought she could live on us alone. Or maybe she is angry with us, now she's realized that isn't the case. We would feel sorry about that. We'd hope what we've done for her already would be enough: giving her body warmth, making life on earth possible. We'd hope she hadn't expected us to render food unnecessary, that she'd taken us for what we were, as we do with her. But there is probably another reason she is crying. She's probably missing someone. Elisabeth, or her friends from college. Or she's missing her dad. That wouldn't surprise us. We saw her expression when she looked at her father, as a child, as a young adult. And we saw how he looked back at her. We'd miss those mutual glances too.

Whatever it is she's crying about, it sets her in motion because she pushes off her fleece blanket and sits upright. She wipes the tears from her eyes. And, glancing at her sleeping housemates, she quietly gets up and tiptoes to a small pile of clothes on the piano stool. She picks up the clothes and takes them into the kitchen. We shine in here all the way from the moon, straight through the elongated window in the back door, forming a silvery white trapezium on the floor and filling the whole room with a white glow. Muriel drops her pyjama bottoms, takes a pair of trousers from amongst her clothes, and puts them on. Her pyjama top comes off; she puts on a vest. On top of this a T-shirt and then a sweater. And even though it's a warm night, she zips it up all the way to the top. She folds up her pyjama bottoms and top and puts the folded clothing in the drawer with the tea towels. Then she feels in her right trouser pocket and gets out a folded piece of paper. She unfolds it and reads what is written there. Her lips move along with the words. Once she's finished, she folds the sheet once and slides it half under the slow juicer. From her back pocket she takes a white pen with the logo of the police on its side. She writes *For*

Petrus and Melodie on the part of the paper sticking out from under the slow juicer. She puts the pen down next to the juicer, leans forward, and presses her lips to the side of the appliance. Then she straightens up, looks around the kitchen once again, and creeps back to the living room where the others are still asleep. Keeping one eye on her housemates, she goes over to the table upon which is a small filing cabinet with four drawers. Her name is written on the bottom drawer. She pulls it open slightly and glances aside. She pulls it a little further open. And a little further. Melodie, who is lying facing Muriel, lets out a deep sigh and turns onto her other side. Muriel freezes. She remains rigid for a few seconds, then she lets her shoulders drop. She opens the drawer fully and takes some papers from it, which she folds and puts in her back pocket. Then she closes the drawer in a single movement and turns back to her housemates. Her hands in her pockets, she studies them lying there next to each other on their airbeds with her bed next to theirs, the blanket pushed back as though she might slide into it at any moment, and unlike earlier, she now looks like she does want to see things. Her sleeping housemates beneath their fleece blankets, the sofa, in our feeble presence not red but dark grey, the pile of four meditation cushions next to the sofa, the lutes on the wall, the viola da gambas, the butterflies, the cork noticeboard with the roster of who can use the laptop when. She gives each object her full attention for a few long seconds. Then she turns and goes into the hall. She quietly opens the door and closes it behind her. She pauses for a moment, feeling in the pockets of her sweater. Squeezes her eyes shut as though she's forgotten something. She looks from the door to the stairs and then back to the door. She chooses the stairs, quietly going upstairs, avoiding the fifth and the eleventh step. At the top she goes into a room with a single bed covered in piles of sheet music, and a large wardrobe. She opens the wardrobe and takes a weekend bag from the bottom shelf. She smells the bag and smiles. Then she begins to fill it with items of clothing. In the bathroom she takes a toothbrush from the glass on the washstand. Without making a noise she reads the note attached to the side of the mirror. She looks at herself. Her eyes seem even more sunken in their sockets than usual, but this doesn't seem to bother Muriel. She smiles at herself, nods, and goes back into the other room to put her toothbrush in the bag. She goes down the stairs, the bag over her shoulder, avoiding the eleventh and fifth steps.

Downstairs in the hall she puts down the weekend bag. She looks at the door. The little curtain in front of the door's pane of glass. The wind chime above the door, a wooden disk with thin metal tubes of differing lengths. The wind chime that doesn't hang outside in the wind but inside the front door so that there's always music when anyone enters or leaves. Hung there by Muriel herself one sunny October day. The same day they'd hung up their nameplates next to the front door.

"Nice, isn't it?" she'd said. "Nice, isn't it, Melodie? Anyone coming or going will be greeted with Sounds. And Love, too, of course."

"Yes, very nice, Muriel. Sweet of you to add a piece of yourself. I think it's a nice initiative. Don't you, Petrus? Elisabeth?"

Over the months after that, we saw Muriel smile every time she heard the wind chime tinkle. She looked at it as though it were a friend of hers. But now she looks at it as though it is a source of doubt. She turns back to the living room door, and then to the wind chime. Then she goes back upstairs, skipping the fifth and the eleventh, and along the hall to the bathroom where she takes a first-aid kit from the cupboard and gets a pair of scissors from it, which she puts point upwards in her trouser pocket. She gets a plastic stool from under the washbasin and goes back downstairs. She puts the stool in front of the door beneath the chimes, gets a scarf from the hat stand, and stands on the stool. It's slightly too low for her to be able to reach properly but if she stands on her toes she is able to bind the chimes together with the scarf in a single movement so that the sound arising is immediately muffled. Holding the chimes in the scarf with her left hand, she gets the scissors out of her pocket with her right. She reaches as high as she can, trying to cut the threads attaching the wooden disk to the central suspension cord. She snips a few times and misses but finally she manages it. The wind chime is free. She puts it, wrapped in the scarf, on the shoe rack under the hat stand. She puts the scissors on top and sets the stool at the bottom of the stairs. She gets her coat from the stand and puts it in the weekend bag. Then she puts on her shoes. She does up the laces with trembling fingers. She stands up, hangs the bag over her shoulder, and puts her hand determinedly on the front door's latch.

The door doesn't open. Muriel moves the latch up and down a few times as she tries to push open the door, but it remains closed. She looks back over her shoulder at the living-room door. The keys are behind that door, hanging on a hook on the side of the bookcase. Again she begins to cry, not as quietly and subtly as just now with just a few tears that leave pretty glittering trails on her sad but serene face, but full force now, with jerking shoulders and a face drawn with pain. She sinks to her knees and then lies down on the floor in between the two triangular orange patches we project onto the carpet. She closes her eyes and lies there until the crying has stopped. Then she gets up. She stands with her face to the wall. To her left the front door, to her right the door to the living room, diagonally behind her the stairs. Her legs orange to about half way up, the rest in darkness, but not in so much darkness that she's no longer visible.

This is how far she has come. The hall. The front door that is locked. And it doesn't matter to us what happens next, whether she goes back in to the living room to get the keys from the hook before returning to the hall to leave by the front door, or whether she leaves the house through the garden door in the kitchen and climbs over the fence, or whether Petrus or Melodie wake up when she enters the living room, and whether they persuade her to stay, or whether she doesn't even dare tell them she was planning on leaving, so that she'll have to invent an excuse about a text message sent to the house telephone, that her father is dying, or whether she remains standing here, conflicted, until morning comes, or whether she decides to stay, hang the chimes back up as well as she can, take off her shoes, take her things back upstairs, and lie back down under her fleece blanket with her clothes on in the hope that she'll have been able to invent a good explanation for why she's wearing her normal clothes and not her pyjamas. You won't hear us expressing a point of view. We only want to leave you observing this scene: viewed from the living-room door, the profile of a woman, dark against the hour-glass-shaped curtain on the door; viewed from the front door a woman's face illuminated orange, with traces of tears on her cheeks, turning now fully to the orange light, and then back to the living-room door. A woman, caught in an in-between space, purgatory, neither outside nor inside, and each time a car drives down the street and a shaft of pale yellow headlamp light comes into the hall, she raises her eyebrows and shrugs, and when the light has gone again, she lets them drop and returns to her inner conflict.

We won't have an opinion about what she decides to do. The choice is hers, your task is to observe it. All we can do is stay with her, light up her face, stroke her hands, make sure that everything is seen.

Acknowledgements and sources

In the writing of this book I was inspired by the news of a woman's death in a suburb of Utrecht in the summer of 2017. I have made use of newspaper articles and information given online, including the commune's website. I have never seen or spoken to those involved and it wasn't my intention to make any judgements about the real-life events or people. The story I have written is the product of my imagination and should be read as fiction.

The quote in the chapter "We are the parents" comes from the cover of the Dutch translation of Rachel Carlson's book, *Silent Spring*.

Various people have helped me in the writing of this novel. I would like to thank Janneke Burggraaff and Michel Heen for answering my questions about the practical side of their work as GP and police officer. I would like to thank Jan-Tjeerd de Jong from the Rotterdam police for his warm welcome at the police station and for his feedback on an earlier version of the story. I am particularly grateful to Uitgeverij Podium and my editor, Willemijn Lindhout for their unrelenting enthusiasm for my work and their careful guidance during the completion of the manuscript. And finally I would like to thank all the people I have shared a house with for what they have taught me about love, conflict, and (in)difference.

For the English edition I would like to thank the World Editions team, Judith Uyterlinde for making the book accessible to an English readership, translator Michele Hutchison for her smooth and inventive translation, and Lydia Unsworth & Robin Shimanto Reza for finetuning the text.

The translator would like to thank classical musician and translator Eileen Stevens for checking the musical sections of the translation for accuracy.

MICHELE HUTCHISON studied at UEA, Cambridge, and Lyon universities and worked in publishing for a number of years. In 2004, she moved to Amsterdam. Among the many works she has translated are *Grand Hotel Europa* by Ilja Leonard Pfeijffer, *Fortunate Slaves* by Tom Lanoye, both *Craving* and *Roxy* by Esther Gerritsen, and *Stage Four* by Sander Kollaard, for which she received the Vondel Translation Prize 2020. In the same year, her translation of Marieke Lucas Rijneveld's novel *The Discomfort of Evening* was awarded the International Booker Prize. She also co-authored the successful parenting book, *The Happiest Kids in the World*.

Book Club Discussion Guides on our website.

World Editions promotes voices from around the globe by publishing books from many different countries and languages in English translation. Through our work, we aim to enhance dialogue between cultures, foster new connections, and open doors which may otherwise have remained closed.

Also available from World Editions:

The Leash and the Ball
Rodaan Al Galidi
Translated by Jonathan Reeder
"Al Galidi has an eye for the absurd."
—*Irish Times*

Cocoon
Zhang Yueran
Translated by Jeremy Tiang
"An intricately crafted web of secrets."
—*Publishers Weekly*

Tale of the Dreamer's Son
Preeta Samarasan
"Samarasan's inventive prose is stunning."
—*The Guardian*

Abyss
Pilar Quintana
Translated by Lisa Dillman
"Small details that can define an entire continent."
—*Vogue*

The Gospel According to the New World
Maryse Condé
Translated by Richard Philcox
"Condé has a gift for storytelling."
—*New York Times Book Review*

On the Design

As book design is an integral part of the reading experience, we would like to acknowledge the work of those who shaped the form in which the story is housed.

Tessa van der Waals (Netherlands) is responsible for the cover design, cover typography, and art direction of all World Editions books. She works in the internationally renowned tradition of Dutch Design. Her bright and powerful visual aesthetic maintains a harmony between image and typography, and captures the unique atmosphere of each book. She works closely with internationally celebrated photographers, artists, and letter designers. Her work has frequently been awarded prizes for Best Dutch Book Design.

The background image on the cover is a photograph of some orange peel by Frans Toet, taken with a special macro lens. The oranges photographed in this session, despite being from the same batch, all had quite different skins: their dots appeared either as dimples or spheres of light, and the density of the dots also differed. We chose the most juicy and glowing, to represent light, despite the fact that it is a dried orange peel which features in the novel. The font is Didonesque Display by Paolo Goode, 2017.

The cover has been edited by lithographer Bert van der Horst of BFC Graphics (Netherlands).

Euan Monaghan (United Kingdom) is responsible for the typography and careful interior book design.

The text on the inside covers and the press quotes are set in Circular, designed by Laurenz Brunner (Switzerland) and published by Swiss type foundry Lineto.

All World Editions books are set in the typeface Dolly, specifically designed for book typography. Dolly creates a warm page image perfect for an enjoyable reading experience. This typeface is designed by Underware, a European collective formed by Bas Jacobs (Netherlands), Akiem Helmling (Germany), and Sami Kortemäki (Finland). Underware are also the creators of the World Editions logo, which meets the design requirement that "a strong shape can always be drawn with a toe in the sand."

CPSIA information can be obtained
at www.ICGtesting.com
Printed in the USA
JSHW082103270523
42354JS00002B/2